RENTAL

Boston Rebels, book 6

RJ SCOTT

V.L. LOCEY

Love Lane Books

Copyright

Rental (Boston Rebels #6)

Copyright © 2023 RJ Scott, Copyright © 2023 V.L. Locey

Cover design by Meredith Russell, Edited by Kathy Krick

Published by Love Lane Books Limited

ISBN - 9781785645914

All Rights Reserved

Rental (Boston Rebels, 6)

A steamy romance between a player and a referee breaks all the rules but will it destroy everything?

Five different cities in eight years — Logan's never had the chance to settle in one place. He's the guy who fills in gaps on teams as a temporary fix and is traded at year's end because no one wants to keep a thirty-year-old rental after he's outlived his usefulness. When he's called up to the Rebels, he knows it's his last run in the NHL. Now, he must decide if it's worth carrying on with the weight of his secrets around his neck for one more year. He's never had a love that mattered, his career is nearly done, his ex-wife is remarrying, his sex life is drier than a desert, and abruptly, Logan's had enough. He craves one night to ease the frustration, and hooks up with someone tall, dark, and dangerous in the bathroom of a club. The sex is off the charts, but it's one and done, until Logan realizes exactly who he slept with and understands how dangerous it is to play games with secrets.

Being a referee is in Webber's blood, and it's a job he loves. Sure, sometimes he's called dirty names—by fans, coaches, and players—or must insert himself between two massive men trying to pummel each other. Some nights, he's knocked on his ass. Other times, he might take a puck to a tender spot. But despite all the hazards and name calling, there is no place he wants to be than on the ice. If only his love life was as settled. It's hard to find someone willing to put up with his travel schedule, and even if he found Mr. Right, how would he juggle a romance when he's never home? A chance hookup while officiating a game in Boston should be a simple matter of scratching that itch, but he couldn't be more wrong. Unfortunately, that one-night stand—while memorable—turns his sedate life upside down in ways he could've never foreseen. When the penalty for love is losing everything he's worked hard for, is it a price he's willing to pay?

Dedication

To my family who accepts me and all my foibles and quirks. Even the plastic banana in my holster.
VL Locey

Always for my family.
RJ Scott

RENTAL
BOSTON REBELS BOOK 6

RJ SCOTT &
V.L. LOCEY

Love Lane Books

Chapter One

Webber

"Mary and her sweet little donkey, February in Boston is frigging cold," I muttered as I hustled down an icy sidewalk past the Common, head bowed to stop the ice pellets from sandblasting the skin on my face. The wind howling across the famed park tore at my clothing, ripping at the scarf I'd tied around my face after leaving the barn. "I must be fucking insane to be out in this kind of weather. Stupid dick."

My cock, which was now burrowed up into my body with my balls, seeking warmth, remained silent. For once. Let it never be said that a man who'd just turned forty had no sex drive. Not that I said that, but I heard kids online talking as if once you hit forty you turned into the Crypt Keeper. I still had a ravenous sex drive. Thank you very much Gen X, or whatever Gen we were now dealing with. Drive was not the issue. Lack of time to act on my wants was. Also, it was tricky to be an NHL ref and find a secretive place to hook up with a guy. My face was kind of well-known in all the hub cities. Lots of fans liked me when I made calls that went for their team. When I made calls that went against them, they hated me. But I did keep them entertained on the ice, or tried to, and the league, as well as the fans and players, enjoyed my theatrical nature. Not that the league cared much about gay officials. They'd become quite tolerant, and even downright welcoming, to LGBTQ players over the past ten or so years. The bigwigs wouldn't have batted an eye over a queer ref. There were so many out players now. Thanks in large part to Tennant Madsen-Rowe, who had been gutsy enough to come out publicly.

No, my being silent about my queerness wasn't because I feared backlash from the league. My choice to keep my sexuality on the DL, as the hip kids say, was because it was simply easier to keep my private life private. This way, there was that much less for fans to bitch about when I made a call they didn't care for. And trust me, that happened a lot. It's a wonder every child of an NHL official doesn't think his or her name has sucks attached to it because that's what I hear at least ten times per night. Hell, some fans throw dead fish at the officials. You've not lived until you have had a warm, slimy catfish slap you in the face. We won't even talk about the octopus tossing that takes place in a certain city.

A gust blew down the street as I waited to cross. Why on earth were so many people outside at midnight in this town? Did they not grasp that the city was under siege from a winter storm that would drive the Watch from the Wall? Bostonians are a rough breed. And that acknowledgment comes from a boy born and raised in Georgetown, Ontario. Webber Kelty is not some sunbird from the Florida Keys. I spent my childhood sledding, playing hockey, and drinking Mom's homemade chicken noodle soup from a thermos alongside frozen ponds. Dressing in layers was as natural to my twin brother and me as was skating. What with Dad being a hockey referee as well, Trevor and I grew up in the sport.

"Thanks," I shouted into the wind when a kind soul took pity on me and let me dash across the street. Bet he didn't know who I was behind this scarf with my toque pulled down to my eyebrows. If they did, and they were a Rebels fan, they'd have run me over for that call I made on the Boston captain the last time I had been called into town to officiate a game. Hey, tripping is tripping. I don't care if you wear the C or not, if you jam your stick into someone's skate right in front of me, you're getting the call and doing the time. Boston fans had long memories. As did New York fans. Just ask Denis Potvin.

I pulled out my phone after crossing the street, wiped the sleet from the screen, and checked my map again. Yep, ahead and down a side street. I forded on, the wind lashing at me. My eyelashes were frozen as I skidded along the sidewalk to Captain Curly's Cabaret, a tiny place that Google had found for me. It sat back in a skinny alleyway with no sidewalk. Picking my way down the cobblestone walkway, my eyes gazed upon a small neon beer sign— *Samuel Adams*, naturally—blinking. I followed that happy little beacon to a yellow door. Above the door was a wooden sign whipping about in the raucous winds. I blinked to clear the ice crystals from my lashes. Yep, that was a pirate captain with flowing red curls holding a lyre. Cool.

I was met at the door by a burly guy with a lanyard and a grotesque half mask of a demon of some sort.

"Five-dollar cover charge," he informed in a thick accent that lacked any Rs whatsoever. I coughed up the note. He tucked it into a fanny pack, then stood there staring at me. I stared back.

"Is there anything else?" I asked of the behemoth.

"Where's your mask?" I must have looked confused. "It's Mardi Gras night." He pointed to a poster on the backside of the stout wooden door. Ah. Yeah, so I see. Mardi Gras Night. Cool. "Everyone has to wear a mask, or they're not allowed in."

"Oh, well, I don't have a mask on me."

He rolled weary eyes, then picked up a ratty box full of various masks. "Pick one. Return it when you leave. Don't get booze, food, or jizz on it." My eyes rounded. "Shit happens. Pick one. I got other people to attend to." I glanced behind me and found only the door with the poster. He arched a thick eyebrow when I looked back at him. "I didn't say them people was behind you."

No, he did not. Shame on me. I reached into the box and pulled out a pink flamingo half mask. The feathers were a little worn and several were bent. I took a moment to inspect it.

"How sanitary is this?" I asked, holding the mask up by its elastic string. He sighed wearily, bent down, stood up with a can of Lysol, and gave the mask a dousing.

"Anything else, Monk?" he asked, sarcasm dripping from each word.

"Nope." I grinned, pulled the flamingo mask over my head, and stepped around the grumpy doorman.

I pushed into the bar, sighing at the rush of warmth, as well as the smell of deep fryer grease. My stomach gurgled. I hadn't had a chance to eat after my late flight from Pittsburgh. Rumor had it that Boston had some damn fine chowder. Rumor being everyone in the city telling you that Boston had *damn fine chow-dahhh.* I'd been here enough times in my career to know that the chowder claim was true. Standing just inside the door, I shook off the melting ice pellets as I took in the bar. It was a nice place. Dark wooden bar filled with patrons, blue walls, red ceiling, nicely buffed wooden flooring, and tables packed with diners. There were several TVs on the walls, but none of them were on ESPN or NESN.

A few men looked my way, sizing me up. My cock decided it was time to wiggle free of my torso as it found men. Lots of men. Mostly nice-looking men. Well, as nice-looking as one could be in a Mardi Gras mask. They all had attractive lower faces anyway.

I made my way to the bar, eager to have a hot man, a cold beer, and a warm meal. Preferably in that order, but if the food and beer came first, I was okay with that. My dick might not be, but he could just chill. He'd managed to sit out any social activities for a few weeks now. With the season in full swing, we officials traveled a lot. I mean like a lot a lot.

At the moment, the league had roughly thirty-five or so officials on the payroll. We're assigned in pairs to officiate games throughout the season with multiple trips across the US/Canadian border. Last year, I officiated seventy games.

I missed a couple due to catching the flu. That was twelve games less than an NHL team plays each regular season. We zebras were all about those frequent flyer miles. Granted, we did receive travel stipends from the league and a nice salary. Not as much as the players, but with my tenure, I was pulling in a fat sum of about four-hundred thousand a year, plus playoff bonuses if we're selected. I was comfortable.

And being a bachelor meant that all my money stayed in my bank account, aside from a mortgage payment and the other monthly bills. I had no kids and no husband. Which had started to niggle at me a little when I'd hit the big 4-0 last summer. My family was quick to remind me I was not getting any younger—cheeky of my twin to say that—and perhaps it was time to stop being a hockey vagabond and settle down with a nice guy. Adopt a kid or two. Get a dog. Like Trevor and his husband, Carl, had done. My brother and his amazing family were making me look bad.

Pulling out a stool, I removed my coat, draped it over the back of the seat, and hoisted my backside up. With a sigh, I planted my rump, checking out the tidy bottles of booze lined up along the wall. The barkeep arrived, a good-looking guy in a yellow polo with matching Tweety Bird earrings. His shirt bore the redheaded pirate on the front.

"Samuel Adams, please, and a menu?" I asked. He nodded, moved off to pull me a beer and grab a menu. Raking my fingers through my short, damp brown hair, I settled in, looked to the left, and saw one of the most gorgeous men I'd ever seen before, staring at me as if I were a bacon cheeseburger, and he was just coming out of a meat-free Lent drought. Gorgeous lower half of his face, anyway. He wet his lips. My pecker perked up instantly. I barely noticed the beer and menu that appeared in front of me. The bartender, who was probably used to seeing men drooling on his bar, moved off to tend to his other customers. "Evening," I said, because I was smooth and suave that way.

"Hey," he replied, his voice deep as the ocean depths. He was dirty blond, big, and inked. Also, a little younger than me. Not by eons or anything, but maybe early thirties. He had a rugged face, a nose that was wider and, perhaps, a wee bit crooked. Incredibly lush lips, and one hell of a strong jaw. Dark blue eyes. That nose/jaw combo was a real standout. His face was rough and masculine, but he'd not be appearing on the cover of any high-fashion magazine. The man was not a fashionable waif. He was a bruiser. And just my type. His mask was purple with sequins. Very flashy for a man who didn't strike me as the flashy type, but then again, what did I know about him other than my dick was into his vibe. "You here for food or something else?"

My dick was standing at attention. Okay then, the straightforward type. "I'm here for whatever the night brings me."

He gave me a smile that could have jarred Satan. Talk about sinful. "Yeah, same." With that announcement, he slid from his stool, adjusted his cock, which looked like a thick hunk of meat pressing against the zipper of his jeans, and sauntered off. I sat there overwhelmed, not only at the quickness of finding a willing fuck, but at the potential sheer size of that man's cock. His ass was a work of perfection. Meaty as hell. Damn this bar was a treasure trove! Why had I not googled gay bars in Boston when I was here before?! He paused at the end of a dark hallway, bathroom signs lit above his head, and gave me that look. That look that scorched all my nerve receptors aside from the ones that led to my crotch. He walked off into the dimly lit corridor.

The bartender cleared his throat. I glanced at him, waiting with a pencil and pad in his hand.

"I have to go wash up first," I lied like a motherfucking rug.

"Uh-huh." He placed the pad back into his front pocket and went to make cocktails.

Feeling a little ashamed of how obvious this whole thing was, I nonetheless left my beer behind, trying to appear nonchalant as I moseyed down that shady corridor. I passed a swinging door to the kitchen, then a door to what I assumed was a storage closet of some kind. On the left were the bathrooms. One for the ladies, one for the gents. I slipped into the men's room. Mr. Magnificent stood by a stall, his eyes hooded, his hand resting on the door to keep it open.

"You're hot," he muttered.

I blinked at his comment. Such a straightforward fellow. Not that fucking in a bathroom had to be flowery, but maybe he could have opened with something less direct.

"Thanks. You are as well."

Jerking his head at me, he beckoned me to enter the stall. I did as requested, pressing around him, our chests rubbing as I slithered into the stall. I gave the area a fast once over. It was clean. Enough. God, was this really where I was now at this stage of my life? Honestly, there had to be something better. Kneeling in a puddle of piss was not exactly romantic.

He closed the door, latched it, and then slipped his big hands around me, tugging my backside into his groin.

Holy. Shit. The man was packing. How did he manage to walk with a jumbo Swiss Colony meat log in his BVDs? He rutted against my ass as he buried his face into my neck. My cock was freed deftly, and he took hold of me, stroking me with rough fingers. His whiskers abraded my neck as he nibbled silently, his hips rolling steadily.

"I want to fuck you," he growled into my flesh.

"Yes, please, okay, yes, let's do that," I said, my brain having left my cock in charge of things for a moment. Be right back. Dicking about to commence. Thanks for stopping by.

With a speed that did not match up with his size, he had my pants and briefs down around my ankles in no time.

"Sweet ass," he commented, his words vibrating through my jugular to rush through my body with each pump of blood. "I'm going to fuck you good."

"Yes… please…" I closed my eyes, placed my hands on the cold metal wall of the stall, and spread my legs as much as I could manage. The sound of his zipper going down made my dick leak. I heard the tear of a foil packet, then felt the fluttery sensation of said packet tracking down my spine before falling to the floor.

"Hurry," I grunted as he tore into another packet. Lube,

I hoped, because there was no way that monstrous cock of his was going inside me without slippery assistance. "Use more lube."

"Only got two packets," he replied, his voice as smoky as a side of bacon.

"Use them both. You're massive," I replied, letting my brow rest on the stall as he ripped into another packet. His fingers were chilly as they found my hole. Fat and thick, they breeched me, working lube into me. For that, I was grateful. "Thanks," I managed to cough out right before his dick replaced those beefy fingers.

"Such a sweet ass," he growled and snapped his hips forward. I yelped at the invasion. The burn was monumental, but so damn good at the same time. "Hold on," he huffed. "It'll only hurt for a few seconds."

"Right," I ground out, amazed that I could speak with his cock resting on my tonsils.

He began to move, slowly, praise all the gay gods, and within a few thrusts, my body had adjusted to him, more or less. His thighs bumped mine as his fingers dug into my hips.

"God... above... so good," I whimpered before spitting into my palm. Taking my dick in my fist, I began pumping. Mr. Magnificent picked up the pace. Skin slapped skin, grunts and huffs floated upward from our stall, and the sounds of the jukebox playing faded away. All I heard was the thundering of my heart, the sensual sounds of two men fucking, and the thump of my brow against the wall of the stall. I'd have a headache soon. Totally worth it. A man didn't get... fucked like this... Jesus Christ... every day.

"You close?" he asked with a growly sort of exhalation that was crazy sexy.

"So… close," I panted, tugging on the head of my dick as if it were taffy. "I think… you're going to… split me in half."

"Nah, baby… you can take it." He let go of my hip to give my bare ass cheek a loving little pat, then surged into me with a brute power that stole my breath. I shot all over my hand, crying out in pure bliss as he pounded my poor ass for all it was worth. "Shit… so tight."

He rose onto his toes to go deeper, his hand rising to take hold of my hair. The string snapped and my mask fell to the floor of the stall. At this point, I could not have cared less.

"Shit. Sorry," he grunted, twisting my head around to kiss me on the mouth. "Going deeper, hold on. I'm going to come."

Deeper?! Fucking hell his cockhead was poking my brain, and the bastard wanted to get deeper?! Shit yes. Yes, he did, and it was glorious. More spunk flew out of me, speckling the wall, dripping out from between my fingers and probably landing on top of my shoes. Did not give two damns. His orgasmic roar sent shudders through me. It was primal and masculine. I whimpered as another spurt of cum flew from me. I caught it, rubbed it over the head of my prick, and shivered with delight.

"Such a sweet ass," he whispered hoarsely, pulling out quickly and bending over my bowed back to drop a kiss on the nape of my neck. "You okay?"

"Muhah," I replied as I did my best to not collapse to the floor in a heap. "Fine… great fuck."

"Yeah, it was." He bit down on the back of my neck. My skin prickled. The bite was just hard enough to titillate. The condom hit the crapper, and he flushed it down and zipped his pants. "See you around."

"Totally," I said as I bent down to reach for my pants, which were around my ankles. Ouch. Ow. Oh fuck. I'd be feeling that dick inside me for days. Skating tomorrow night would be fun. Not. The latch on the door brought my head up and around just in time to see him walking out. Then, the door swung shut in my face. Moving a bit more slowly, I eased my underwear and pants up, wincing as I took a few steps. Shit, that was some dicking. I'd better stop at a drugstore on the way home to find something soothing for my poor little butthole. I took time to wash my hands because who knew what was on the walls in that...

Oh. I ran back into the stall with some soapy paper towels to clean off my mess and pick up my broken mask. I dropped the whole lot into a trash can, then washed my hands once more. I chanced a look at myself in the mirror. Oh yeah, I looked like I had just been reamed by a Clydesdale. After wetting my hands and smoothing down my hair, I made my way back to my seat. My gait was decidedly western. When I eased my backside down onto the stool, the bartender was watching me.

"I'm ready for something to eat now," I said, my voice a little reedy.

"I bet you are." He slid a green mask—a frog this time —over the bar.

Heat raced into my face as I pulled the mask on without sanitizing it. I ordered something filling and greasy, then slunk down on my stool to nurse my beer. No one in this gay bar seemed to care that I'd just had my brains fucked out of me. Maybe they couldn't tell.

"They sell stuff for your asshole down the street at the twenty-four-hour pharmacy." My gaze flew from my Samuel Adams to the guy on my left. "Get the ass cream in the blue tube. Works wonders and makes your pucker smell like mint julep."

"Blue tube of ass cream. Mint juleps. Got it." I gave him a measly thumbs up, slithered down into my chair even further, and thanked all the gods that no one—other than this guy and the bartender—would ever know about what just took place in that stall. Oh, and Mr. Magnificent. But I'd likely never see him or his incredible cock ever again.

Chapter Two

Logan

"Jeez, Chloe, what are they doing?" I tried to peer past my sister at my nieces standing behind her. She shot them a quick glance so hard the phone wobbled and, for a moment, all I had was a view of my sister's ceiling.

"I was on late shift last night," she said and yawned. She was a trauma nurse and constantly worked different shifts, but somehow she and her husband, Dave, made it work as a family.

"And that means?"

"They have pasta and paint, and I can't even right now," she muttered as she tucked her dark hair behind her ear. "My oh-so-thoughtful husband said he'd give me time to read, and said he had them doing crafts, then he got called into work, and that means..." She waved at the chaos behind her. I loved Dave. He was a good guy, the kind of man that a brother always hoped would marry their sister. He was patient and kind and thoughtful, and an engineer with a solid and steady career, who'd swept Chloe off her feet in fifth grade and proposed at senior prom. People said they wouldn't last, but people were wrong, and fifteen years later, with my nieces Amy and Dawn adding to the family, their marriage was impossibly perfect. "I will kill him when he gets home," she added, and then rolled her eyes. "Although, he promises he's bringing home takeout, so I may have to kiss him to death for that."

"He knows how to get around you."

She smiled. "So, are you ready for tonight?"

"Yeah, I'm at the arena already."

She rested her chin on her fists and smiled at me. "Color me surprised. How early are you this time?"

"Ninety minutes, give or take."

"Who are you playing tonight?"

"I'm wounded you don't know," I teased and received another eye roll for my comment. "Carolina's in town."

"Oh! Carolina! I love that big guy, y'know, the one who checked you into the boards that time. The tall one with the eyes."

"Lucerne," I reminded her as I recalled that particularly crushing hit and winced. "Anyway, I'm sitting in my car, waiting for the rest of the guys to arrive, and I thought I'd call my big sister, no special reason at all." *Liar. I need to tell someone what I did last night.*

"Hmmm." She peered at me as much as you could through a phone. "You look tired. Are you okay?"

"Of course, I am. Do I need a reason to call you?" *Nope, I fucked this stranger at a bar, and I'm freaked out over breaking all my personal rules, and I just needed to see your face to remind myself I have someone in my corner.* She didn't get a chance to answer because my youngest niece was waving something at me.

"Look, Uncle Logan! It's for you!" Little Dawn held up a piece of cardboard with pasta stuck in patterns, and I did all the right things that uncles do. I looked on in awe and I made all the right noises, and she added it carefully to the pile for me to pick up the next time I visited. Not that this would be soon, given they were in Nova Scotia, and I was in Boston. Way back, Dave had gotten work up there, and my sister had gone with him. I was drafted down to Florida and headed south, and since then, I hadn't stopped moving. My sister was my touchstone—and her home was the one place I knew I could always rest my head.

"Uncle Lo, is you a'mental?" Amy asked, climbing up into her mom's lap.

"A mental?" I glanced at her mom, who shrugged.

"Daddy said you're a mental."

I blinked at my sister, and she blinked back, and then it made sense.

"I'm a rental," I said with a laugh, emphasizing the R at the beginning of the word. "Not mental." Although that was open for debate, given I strap knives to my feet and fly around a rink at top speed trying to avoid getting hurt.

"Was'a rental?" she asked, and that was a leading question. A rental was me. I'm that guy that a team will trade for at the deadline for the express purpose of a one-time run into the playoffs, which were coming up. Washington didn't want me, Boston did, and that was why I was here. My last year of playing professional hockey, and the upside was that I was lucky to be picked up by a team actually heading for the playoffs; the downside was the reason I was here, filling a hole left by Moral "Dunny" Dunkirk who'd retired after a terrible accident. Dunny and I had made our peace when I joined the team a few weeks ago, but still, the loss was incredibly hard on him and the team. I was replacing a fan favorite, brought up to fill that space and help the team win a Cup.

No pressure then. Not the reason I needed to go searching for sex either. Nope. No pressure at all.

"A rental is someone who plays for a lot of teams." I pulled my thoughts back to the answer and explained it to my three-year-old niece, who was patting glue into her hair. "Uhm, Chloe, should Amy be doing that?"

"No, Amy." Chloe eased the sticky hand away and smiled with exasperation at my oldest niece. "I need to go, little brother, have fun."

We said quick goodbyes, and suddenly, I was bereft. Again. I'd been in Boston a few weeks now, but nothing had changed. I was always first for any practices or games because it gave me time to settle myself down. Rentals were either the saviors of the team that needed them or the reason the team failed—there wasn't any in-between. Learning the team's plays and methods on the fly was hard enough but understanding where I fit in was sometimes impossible. Now, I could slouch down in my car and take advantage of the ninety minutes I had to kill and think and plan and chill. I was early for a reason, just so I could see the others arrive, watch dynamics, and figure out things— like friendships, relationships, and what the guys were like —before they went into the practice arena and were on show. Some might say it was creepy staring. I liked to look at it as surveillance that was a means to an end.

First to arrive was Coach Franks, who strode into our practice arena with great confidence. And why wouldn't he be confident? The Rebels had put up a good run of games, sitting nicely at second in the Metropolitan division, and fourth overall out of all thirty-two teams. Losing Dunny had been a shock to the system from which pundits thought the team would never recover, but if anything, it pulled the team together in ways that surprised everyone. The Rebels had moved Austin Rowe to fill his leaving, and abruptly there was space centering their fourth row—they were missing a key piece of their lineup, and that's where I'd come in. I hadn't directly replaced Dunny's position in the lines at all, just filled a hole in the roster, and that's the line I'm sticking to.

The rental. The skater who was brought in toward the end of a season to assist in a Cup run and fill holes. *Not holes in willing guys in bathrooms.*

Fuck, he'd been so perfect—the right height, willing to take my cock, and... one and done. I was getting hard just trying to ignore thinking about it.

Marquis Miller arrived in a long coat, his beanie firmly low on his head, and I watched him walk because he was pure poetry in motion. He was walking in with Oscar Lindros, a bear of a defenseman, who was all growl and bluster and the complete opposite to Marquis. There was something insanely sexy about Marquis, but he was certainly not on the open market now that he'd found Prince Kaleb.

Still, Marquis and Oscar were friendly guys—they all

were. The most time I've ever spent with a team was with Vancouver, a whole two years, but for the most part, I'm with a team for a year or part of the year, and then I'm done. I've been lucky—I've actually picked up the Stanley Cup, pulled into a fiery Washington team at the trade deadline, replaced an injured player, and sacrificed my body on more than one occasion to stop the other team from scoring. I came away from that last game of the Stanley Cup run taking my turn to skate with the Cup, with a fracture in my femur and a dislocated shoulder. But god, it was so worth it.

I think.

The next to arrive was the captain, Xander Holden, the first openly queer captain in the league. I respected the hell out of the guy, coming out, making a statement, putting up with everyone's shit, and still captaining a team reeling from tragedy with Dunny to sitting nicely near the top of the table. No one was quite sure if the Rebels were going to be able to take their winning streak all the way to the playoffs, but the team appeared hungry for it. Everyone said they'd be fighting Washington, but, after a shaky start to the season, their other rivals, the Railers, had fought their way to tuck in right behind Boston in the tables. The way things sat right now, it would be us against the Railers fighting in the first round, and that thought excited me. Of course, I'd played against the Railers before, and I admired them as a team, just as I did the Rebels; both teams with their queer-positive promotions, and their lack of giving a damn when it came to who dated whom outside of the game.

I wasn't exactly in the closet but being bisexual and

having just come out of a six-year marriage to a woman, no one would have cause to think I was anything but the straight-appearing skater they all saw.

Of course, if they'd seen me last night in the bar. Jesus. That had been some action. I'd fallen deep into his eyes and madness consumed me. I wasn't big on picking up strangers in bars, but that man—I'd never wanted someone so much, and I'd stepped over a line. I wasn't the kind of guy to find hookups in random bars. That just wasn't me.

Then what was I doing there in the first place?

The way he'd glanced at me, his soft smile, the way he sat, the size and shape of him—fuck—the smell of him as I bit into his shoulder and fucked him against the wall. Then, when his mask fell, and I saw his face in the gloom of the bathroom lighting, fuck, he'd been so pretty in my arms, shorter than me, wiry, but solid, and he took everything I gave him. He'd wanted it so badly, and I needed it as much as my next breath. The sounds he made…

Inappropriate erection alert.

I couldn't get caught up in replaying last night, not when I swear I still had endorphins from that encounter sparking and fizzing inside me.

I pressed the heel of my hand to my rebellious cock. *Get your big head back on hockey.*

A few more players trickled in, one guy parked his Porsche next to my '67 Shelby GT500 Super Snake, and I could see him checking out my car, same as he did every time, and then sauntering away. There's a reason why the glass in this car is tinted. I got a rush when I could watch people admiring my baby. If someone liked classic cars, then they'd know all about a GT500. Ironically, it was one thing I had in common with Dunny. The former Boston player loved his classic cars, and I still had the magazine where the interviewer had taken a shot of him next to his Ferrari 290. What I didn't have in common with Dunny was the way the two of us were on the ice. I didn't have his phenomenal speed or his insane accuracy, but I *was* a grinder, and that was what the team needed.

I was good enough to fill gaps, even good enough to lift the Cup, just not good enough for a team to want long-term. Washington had dumped me to trade, and the Rebels picked me up on a two-million-dollar contract—a nice way to end a career and more money in Amy's and Dawn's college funds, which my sister didn't even know existed.

Brady, the eldest of the Rowe dynasty and former captain of the Rebels, now a coach, arrived next. The team might have lost the captain in him and his star power, but he hadn't left them entirely, and as an outsider, I could see his influence on the Rebels' style of play even now. He'd always played a canny observant game, but I wondered if it wasn't time for things to be shaken up. Play the same way for too long, and every other team in the division knew exactly where your vulnerable points were. That was another thing about someone who bounced from team to team—we saw things.

Finally, with nearly everyone else there, I sauntered in where Mr. Big Bad Security Guard, aka Jim, checked my shiny security pass with careful deliberation, then waved me in, fist bumping me on my way through. He was always smiling at me, so I guess he thought it was a good thing I'd joined the team, and hey, it's always good to win over the security in any arena.

I stopped outside the door to the locker rooms for a moment, rolled my neck, and flexed my fingers. *I've got this.*

Shoulders back, pulling down my mask of complete confidence, I pushed open the door and walked into the familiar chaos for the optional morning practice. It was easy to see that nearly the entire team was here, despite the optional part given we had a game tonight. I liked that and thought it spoke of the Rebels' leadership group, who engendered respect and instilled a willingness to get as much ice time as possible in each member of the team. Optional skate might be last-minute strategy or just casually skating in circles, testing edges, warming up the muscles by shooting a few pucks, but it wasn't just about that, it was about friendship and teamwork and building something out of individual skaters that took a team all the way to the top.

I felt at home here.

No one expected the Carolina game to be easy—and it wasn't—although we fought hard.

My cubby was next to Austin Rowe, a star of the future —maybe not quite as shiny as his cousin Ten, but he was fast and deadly accurate. Along with Xander at the core, this was a very strong team. I listened to Austin chatter brightly about rainbow tape and sticks, and the fact that he and his boyfriend were hosting a movie night that weekend, and I should consider myself invited. I nodded along, inserting a few words here and there, as I settled into my pre-game routine. Listening to Queen and replaying "Bohemian Rhapsody" three times in a row was the only irrational hockey player thing I did. It wasn't as if a rental could have superstitions based around the team they played for when that team wouldn't be theirs for long. Still, it didn't stop me from joining in with what some of the other guys did—the fist bumps, the stick taps, and the hollering in the tunnel as we headed out on the ice for warmups.

In front of our home fans and a capacity crowd, which was dotted with red and white Carolina jerseys in a sea of black and gold, I corralled a practice puck and skated behind the net, weaving in and out of my fellow players and taking the puck as close to the center line as I could. I acknowledged a couple of the Carolina players as I passed and then swept wide, switching to skating backward, before tossing the puck in the air and stick handling it from whatever unpredictable angle it hit the ice.

I caught one or two posters in the crowd with my name on them, but they were dwarfed by the amount of Austin Rowe signs being waved around. The poor kid had a shit ton of fans. He spent a few moments tossing pucks to a few of them. I skated to a halt next to him and tapped my stick on his calf.

"It's kind of intense?" I'd seen this kind of thing before with the bright stars of the NHL, the pressure to act in a certain way because of the focus that was on a man as young as Austin. He was due to come off his rookie contract at the end of this season, and pundits were already throwing around figures of six or seven million a year to keep him. He was the Rebels' shiny future, and so damn nice with it that he'd be the perfect ambassador for the sport. There must be something in the Rowe genes.

"I love the fans," Austin said and waved at a couple more as we skated together for a moment.

The zebras were out in force—the refs who would be watching us play and making us pay. I skated close enough to check them out, near enough that they would see me and know I was playing. It was a thing I did—smiling at them, acknowledging them, and getting on their good side.

But then…

Fuck.

The bottom fell out of my world.

Chapter Three

Webber

THE OTHER THREE OFFICIALS ON THE ICE FOR THE GAME, I knew well.

Tim Patterson, Louis St. Mark, and Tomas Kinkaid. We had no say in who the chosen officials were. The Commissioner picked each ref, linesman, video goal judge, and all off-ice officials. These three were good guys. Easy going, sharp-eyed, and pleasant to work with. Just like any other job, there were co-workers you got on well with and co-workers you wanted to bitch slap. Tonight, we had a skilled and seasoned lineup.

Tim and Tomas were the linesmen, and Louis and I were the refs. We'd all arrived about thirty minutes early to stretch and dress—I'd had to stretch gingerly after last night's stellar fuck with the Masked Marvel—and do some last-minute things, such as check over the lists of captains and alternates, as well as any game sheets. Then, we'd simply take a few minutes on the ice to skate and check the ice, as well as the netting. We'd make a few passes of the benches to count players to ensure the number on the bench matched the game reports. I liked to double check the timekeeper and other off-ice officials to ensure they were in place and ready to go.

Little things for sure, but they could become big during the game itself. Once things were as we'd like them, we'd just chill on the ice until it was time to officially begin the game. The league did not like us to be lollygagging around with our hands in our pockets, nor did I, so we always tried to look busy. I took my job seriously and always tried my best to be as professional as possible, both on and off the—

My gaze flickered to a big burly man in a Boston jersey staring at me after he made a lazy pass back to the bench. Damn, he was a good-looking bruiser of a guy. That mouth of his was sinful. And that jawline was... familiar. His eyes were round, his lips parted, his grip on his stick slack.

Oh fuck. Oh. Fuck. Oh, fuck to infinity. It was the Masked Marvel. My heart dropped to my skates as we stood there staring at each other. *Fuuuuuck.*

"... hope they don't fuck around too much. Web, you okay?"

My gaze flew from the man who had made me purchase two blue tubes of ass cream last night. And yes, my butthole did smell like mint juleps. So did my fingers after applying it with winces and flinches. Thanks, random bar patron.

"Oh, yeah, fine, Louis. Uhm, who is number 67?" I asked nonchalantly as sweat began to bead up under my helmet and jersey. Not an "oh I've been doing exercise" sweat either. It was a cold "that player and I fucked last night" sweat. "Why do I not know him?"

"Logan Mackie. He's new to the Rebels. Moves around a lot. Typical rental. Solid, not usually a problem. Also, do you know every player in the league?" he asked with an eye roll. "I mean, do you have a mind like a camera?"

No, obviously not. I knew a lot of the guys in the teams. But sure, there were players I didn't know as well as others. Players came and went all the time. Trades, retirements, call-ups, send-downs, and injuries. It would be virtually impossible to know all the over one-thousand players personally, I told myself. Probably Logan Mackie had been east when I'd been west, or north when I'd been south. And if he wasn't on Webber's Most Wanted List, a mental tally of players that tended to skate a fine line with the rules of clean play that I kept a close eye on, or a superstar like Tennant Rowe or Tate Collins, or a captain or alternate that we had a lot of interaction with, he had... well, somehow I'd just not laid eyes on him before.

And yes, officials tended to mentally categorize players. Most were good guys playing the sport they loved. There was a small group that liked to stir the pot. Mouthy and pushy sorts that we tried to keep an eye on. Then, there were some that were flashy, and they stood out because of those insane skills. Some were just grinding it out with their heads down. Mostly, those were defensemen, but not always. Logan Mackie had somehow eluded notice. Maybe, that was why he moved from team to team like Louis had said. Maybe, he was a mediocre player who was overlooked by all. Which would be incredibly sad, but it did happen.

"No, no camera mind," I replied to the French-Canadian who was staring at me as if I had a mongoose doing a dance on my helmet. "I didn't recognize him. What were you saying?"

"I was saying: I hope they do not fuck around after the game because I have a flight to Florida that I must catch, or my wife will have my balls. It's her mother's birthday, and I have to be there. I tell her, Marie, why do you insist I show up to these things when I'm working?"

"Uh-huh," I said, my gaze riveted to Logan. He wet his lips, and something stirred down in my cup. Nope. No way, penis. Not while officiating. "Yeah, wives. I'm going to skate. Over there." I pointed to the penalty box. Louis's bushy eyebrows beetled. "To check out the penalty box attendant. I think his tie is crooked."

Off I went, leaving Louis to stare at my hastily retreating backside. Logan was glued to the ice by the sin bin, alone, gaping. I skated by him, coming to a slow stop by the penalty box.

"Nice tie," I said to the lanky guy sitting in the box. It really wasn't a nice tie at all. It was kind of gaudy, but that would be rude to point out.

"Thanks, my girlfriend's mother got it for me," he said as he tugged at the checkered monstrosity.

"Keep up the good… ties," I said, turned, and gave Logan a curt nod. "It's a good night for hockey," I said to the dumbstruck player with the incredibly kissable mouth.

"Are you okay?"

I nearly leapt out of my skates at the sound of the

penalty box attendant's voice beside my ear. I spun to glower at the poor guy.

"Fix that tie!" I barked, then hauled my ass to the other side of the ice to stand by the benches while the anthem was being sung. I heard little of the song even with my helmet off. I couldn't shake the upset that was churning in my gut. Also, I had to apologize to the penalty box attendant at some point. His tie was not my problem. I mean, yes, it was ugly, but what was more upsetting than a checkered tie with a floral shirt… just no… stop the madness. I shot the men out on the ice a fast look as we sang about banners yet waving. Logan was not out there with the first line, so I chanced a glance at the bench to my right. There he stood with his eyes locked on me as he mouthed along to the national anthem. A blade of heat speared me in the groin. I cleared my throat as I glanced at the crowd, willing myself to get a fucking hold. This was not an issue that couldn't be resolved. I've called games before with players that I'd had previous interactions with.

Oh really? Interactions as in his dick in your ass?

It would be fine. Logan wouldn't want our indiscretion to become public knowledge any more than I did.

"Web, are you going to drop the puck?"

I stared at Louis and the two linesmen staring at me. Then, I looked at the players gathered at center ice. Shit.

"Yep, just making sure everyone was paying attention! Keep it sharp out there!" I shouted, then hustled to the big Rebels logo in the middle of the rink. I gave the two players a nod, the icy cold puck resting in my hand. "Have a good game, gentlemen, and keep it clean."

Robby Devers from Carolina and Marquis Miller from

Boston both gave me a bob of their heads, then bowed down to attack the puck. Drawing in a huge breath to calm my jangled nerves, I tossed the puck to the ice. It took a hearty bounce. I might have put too much mustard on that one. The two men in front of me shouldered each other aside as I skated back to give them room to play the puck. The linesmen were at their positions at the blue lines, and I took the Boston offensive zone, moving down with speed to keep up with the players.

Carolina had won the faceoff and was now buzzing around the Rebels' net. The puck was flipped off the boards and rolled down my way. I jumped over it as several players raced at me. Down the ice, the play went to Louis. The crowd was loud here in Boston. They took their sports super seriously in this town, as most cities did. Despite how rattled I had been seeing the man that I'd hooked up with on the ice with me, I focused on the action at the other end of the ice. We always had to be on our toes. Hockey was a fast and furious game. The Rebels took a wobbly shot on the Carolina net, then lost the puck in the corner. Lines changed, and the puck was carried back into my zone, but an offside was called by Tomas. Linesmen handled all the puck drops other than game starts, period starts, and after a goal.

I lingered in my end, watching the players reconvene. My gaze moved to the Rebels' bench. Logan was seated among his teammates, studying a tablet, his attention on the game. As if a tether reached out to crack him across that slightly off-kilter nose, his head snapped up and his royal blue eyes found me. Not wanting to be that guy—the one who stared and drooled over a onetime screw—I jerked my gaze from his and focused on the game. This was going to be one *long-ass* night.

Somehow, by the sheer grace of a kind and loving God, the Carolina/Boston game ended on time. Boston held on to a one goal lead, but it hadn't been easily done. It had been a close game, with few penalties and good hard checking. No overtime, so Louis could hurry to the hotel to change and make his flight home. I skittered out of the arena like a whipped dog, head down, shoulders up to my ears, cold wind snarling around me as I jumped into the back of an Uber with Louis. He tried to make conversation, and I did my best to appear as if nothing was wrong, but I suspected I failed miserably. When we arrived at our hotel, he gave me a tired farewell and went to his room to pack. Once he was gone, I slogged to my room, bolted the door behind me, and had a good stiff drink. Generally, I avoided hotel room bars. I mean, really, ten bucks for a shot of whiskey was ridiculous, but there were times when a man would give his left nut for a stiff drink. Tonight, was one of those nights. I tore off the protective wrap on one of two glasses atop the fridge and twisted off the cap.

I was so keyed up, I even skipped the ice. Which meant the two fingers of whiskey were warm and undiluted as I tossed them back. The burn made me shudder. I opened another bottle and dumped it into the standard hotel room glass. I'd cover the expense for the booze myself. Toeing off my shoes, I began circling my room, thinking, thinking, thinking. Then cussing, then thinking some more, then cussing yet again. Stewing and fretting over the situation with Logan was stressing me the hell out. I needed to just calm myself down. I knocked back my second drink, put the glass back on the round tray it had been on, and forced myself to sit the hell down.

Right. Seated. Now, to rules. Were there any rules about a ref sleeping with a player? I highly doubted it. Out queer players and officials was a relatively new thing. So that was good. Still, I would need to do some digging into the by-laws and the contracts that the NHLOA has signed. Christ. I rubbed my hands over my face. A stress headache was coming. I could feel it, which would mean a terrible night's sleep that would make the flight to Toronto miserable.

Another hotel room, another night in a city that wasn't my home, another lonely trip. Sometimes I longed for the simple things like a loving partner, a home-cooked meal, and a dog curled up by my feet. None of that was possible with my travel schedule. Normally, I was okay with it, but on nights like tonight, when I had a mind filled with worry, the alienation of my profession got to me. Refs didn't tend to associate with players off the ice. We usually traveled alone, clocking crazy frequent flyer miles, and people called us names when we did arrive at the job. Hell, some folks threw squids. Nothing shows how much you're loved like a cephalopod to the kisser.

Fuck. Was Toronto another Rebels game? It couldn't be, right?

"Ugh, you're becoming melancholy," I chided myself. I was sure it would all work out. I'd simply avoid Logan Mackie. Easy as pie. Not. Pulling out my phone, I checked my assigned games. Excellent. Over the next few months, I was slated to call several Boston games, some in Bean

Town, and some away. Not that many, and not Toronto. No problem. I'd just pretend Logan wasn't there if I was officiating. He was just another big guy in a sweater. We'd pretend nothing had happened, and that would be it. Simple. It was only one fuck. Sure, it had been an incredible fuck that, if I sat the wrong way—or the right way, depending on how I looked at it—I could still feel. "We'll just live in blissful ignorance. Lots of people do that. How hard could it be to bury that memory?"

Chapter Four

Logan

I HAD TO GET OUT OF THE ARENA AS FAST AS I COULD before the referee with chocolate eyes tracked me down and asked me what the fuck I'd done to him. Or what in god's name I'd been thinking about. I could ask him the same thing—how safe was it to let some random stranger fuck you in a bathroom? Didn't he recognize me? He'd never shown that he had. All we'd done all game tonight was stare, and then not stare, and pretend not to stare. If I'd been more concerned about hockey and less about the guy I'd dicked in a bathroom, then maybe, I wouldn't have fallen for some of the shit that Carolina pulled on me. I'd been called twice for tripping, but that had been complete bullshit, and our captain had talked at length with the referees over the veracity of Carolina's claims. I know because I felt Webber's eyes on me during both arguments as Xander berated what had happened.

So yeah, now I wanted to get away fast. I even

imagined how quickly I could shower, dress, and get my ass out of this place, only I hadn't counted on being dragged into a post-game interview.

No one ever wants to interview the rentals, unless said rental does something of note. Maybe we scored an unlikely hat-trick, maybe we checked somebody too hard, or in my case, maybe they got called twice for tripping, which opened up the Rebels to penalty kills when they didn't need them.

"What about the questionable call in the second period, third minute?" Damien Speight asked. He was one of our resident journalists, critical of our failures, but the first to celebrate our successes. He was a nice guy, friendly to the new rental, telling me after my first game that I was exactly what the Rebels needed in their run for the Cup. Tonight, though, he wasn't being supportive of me or the team, instead he was critical of the refereeing, and in particular how it referenced me. Fuck my life—the last thing I need is to be connected to the referee's team of officials right now.

Even if said official had begged me to fuck him harder, and I'd done just that very thing.

Every player has issues now and then with how games are refereed, but it's the captain or his assistants who are the ones to approach refs, not the rest of the team. Still, we all like to think that, down the line, it wasn't us that'd erred, but the officials who'd missed, or maybe seen, something they should or shouldn't have. Of course, it pissed me off that I'd been called for tripping in the second period. Although, even with him on the ice with me, with memories of what we'd done, I didn't feel unsettled when the calls went against us—the linesmen called them, and they had nothing to do with Webber directly. Yeah, I was dismayed that I'd been called out on the tripping, but I hadn't done it, so I had the moral high ground internally, whatever the call.

A good rental can switch teams at the drop of a hat, travel across the country on the whim of the team, and a good rental certainly doesn't get rattled on the ice by anything—not even by the guy he fucked in a bathroom, who was right there in front of him.

Yeah right. I fucked him. In a bathroom. I fucking fucked *the man.*

"The linesman saw what he saw." I shrugged as I answered the interviewer's leading question. "Killing the penalty, then the goal five minutes later cancels out worrying about tripping calls."

"Do you think your captain should have done more? From where I was sitting, there was no tripping." Damien wasn't exactly asking a question, but he left the comment open for me to jump in. *Better luck next time, Damien… should have interviewed someone else because you're getting nothing from me.*

"We're pleased with the win, the team is strong, we pulled together, took the puck to the net, and scored. At the end of the day, we have our win."

"But you ended up with two unnecessary penalty kills, both in incidences of you allegedly tripping a Carolina player. How do you feel about that?"

Shit, he really was not letting this go, and I mentally turned to page two in the hockey players' post-game interview handbook. "We played Rebels hockey, and we won."

He looked at me steadily. I returned his stare, waiting for him to ask me the same question again with a different format—he was that persistent. Luckily, one of the other interviewers—a short irascible ball ache of a man who never appeared happy with me being here on the team—started asking me things. Even though his question was less pointed, he wasn't questioning the calls. He was probing whether I should be on the team at all. Of course, nobody watching the interview would think that, but I knew.

"Do you think your style of play is adding to the team dynamic?" he asked, and I tilted my chin stubbornly at the hidden implication that I was detracting from the team dynamic. There was nothing wrong with my style of play. Asshole. Before I could think of a reasonable putdown, Xander appeared at my side and laid his arm across my shoulder, made some comment about needing me, and dragged me away from the huddle of journalists. He took his captain's responsibilities seriously, patting me on the back and ushering me into the locker rooms. I gave him a grateful nod, and he winked at me before heading back out to the scrum. He got interviewed after every single game— win or lose—but his answer handbook must be ten pages long with variations of "playing Rebels hockey," "getting the puck to the net," "commitment," and "scoring goals."

I'd actually made it to the shower and could envision getting home, but Coach approached me when I still had a towel around my waist and casually asked if I could attend a short meeting in his office. There went my plans of running as fast as I could from the arena.

"Sure thing, Coach." I didn't spend too long wondering what I was being called in for. At least it was too late to trade me now, so whatever happened, I'd be ending this season as a Boston Rebel. Still, there were many reasons Coach could tell me I'd be a healthy scratch leading up to the Cup and into the fight itself. Counting back from ten and going into negative figures, I got dressed methodically and on autopilot. By the time I straightened my shirt and jacket, I was in exactly the right headspace to deal with Coach. My mask of I-don't-give-a-shit was firmly in place.

"Take a seat," Coach Franks said, gesturing to the broken chair sitting opposite his desk. Rumor was that he kept a broken chair, so people didn't stay long, but I wondered if he even knew it was. I perched gingerly at exactly the right angle so as not to end up on my ass and waited for whatever he needed to say.

"Rough calls tonight," he started, and I nodded in agreement. Coach was just about the only person in the world I could be truly honest with about hockey. I wouldn't let my fellow players see how pissed I was because we'd won the game with a lucky bounce and the puck knuckling its way over the Carolina goalie's glove almost by accident.

"Bad calls, but at least we won." *Barely.* He shook his head like he was shaking away the negative tension. "Anyway, the reason I wanted to call you in is because I'm liking your game. You're confident and fast enough to keep up with our top six if pushed."

"Thanks."

"And I like you for the third line. Thoughts?"

Wait. I was allowed thoughts? I chuckled inwardly and hoped that Coach didn't pick up on my bemusement. My career was one long chain of not being able to pass on my thoughts to contribute strategically. I let my skating speak for itself, and if there was something I saw on ice that didn't work—being super observant—I'd make my point known to the players involved, not by telling them, but by showing them. I wasn't a late addition to a team to cause chaos or to become a first-line genius scorer. I'd leave that up to the big boys.

"Happy to go wherever you think I will work for you best," I finally said and waited for him to agree with me, then send me packing. Instead, he sat back in his chair, steepled his fingers, and regarded me thoughtfully.

"I see a lot of things," he observed. "Some good, some bad. I've been watching you, and I know."

He knew. Somehow, he knew I went to that stupid ass bar, and that I'd fucked the referee that had just officiated our game. Maybe, this was good-cop/bad-cop where he played both parts. Suggest I move up a line and reprimand me for fucking up everything. There was probably a detailed rule against players fucking referees, and shit, maybe I should have checked that out. Although I'm not sure when I would have had time to do it between seeing Webber on the ice and ending up in here.

"I'm sorry?" I offered with caution.

He frowned at me. "Apologize for what?" he asked.

"Nothing," I hedged because I'd confused him with the apology thing, so maybe this wasn't about how I'd fucked up.

"Supposedly, you're thinking of retiring this year?"

Supposedly? Given I'd told no one my inner thoughts, I had no idea where that rumor had started, but Coach was a shrewd guy, and instinct told me he was fishing. No coach had ever asked me whether I was thinking of retiring as a way of getting me off a team, so this was a new one. Unsettling. Not as bad as being on the ice with the referee I fucked, but unsettling.

"I haven't really thought about it," I lied. I'm coming up on thirty-one and that's old in hockey terms. The average age of a player retiring had to be late twenties—I should look it up. Of course, some retirements happened because of injury, but often, it was family commitments or just being damn tired.

"The Rebels have space in the cap and, before we go to your agent officially, I'd like you to think about how you might take a commitment to the Rebels forward into next season."

"Next season. Here? Yeah, sounds good." I was happy to agree, in principle, because an unsigned contract was no contract at all. The main issue was that I got a year's contract, and then, if I wasn't needed, I would become an important tool for trading later in the season. I had value, and I knew what I was worth. I'd been lucky so far with the teams that I'd gone to—teams that were fighting for the top—and I'd held the Stanley Cup, and it was addictive. But even though Coach was talking about next year, I knew I didn't want more because what if halfway through next year I got traded to a team that I didn't respect? Then what? Law of averages meant that shit would have to hit the fan one day, and I wasn't standing in the way to get covered in it. I wanted to end my career on a high, and yeah, retirement was right in the middle of my life plans, but I didn't want Coach to have any reason to think I was giving up before we moved into the playoffs.

I will never give up fighting for the team that has me. My loyalty is absolute.

"Good, good," Coach muttered and shuffled some papers, which I took to mean that the meeting was over. "You have questions?"

He was still staring at me, even after shuffling paper, and now I was confused about what I should say next. Maybe I should ask him if there was a rule about players and referees. Then, maybe, find out if either of the parties concerned wore a mask would that negate the rule. Or if there was a rule that meant that if it happened in a bathroom, it didn't count.

I'm getting hysterical. Adrenaline overload.

"No, nothing," I finally said.

This time he shuffled the papers more dramatically. I eased myself off the broken chair, nodded my thanks again, and closed the door behind me after I left. Coach always had an open-door policy. Aside from directly after games. I'd found that out the hard way the first night I played for the Rebels. He called me in to welcome me properly because I'd only landed half an hour before the game, then reamed me out for leaving the door open. New team, new procedures. I was quick at learning.

"We're going for coffee." Austin caught me as I walked to my locker to pick up my bag. I loved the guy, loved playing with him, loved hearing his stories about how happy he was with Robbie, but honestly, could there be any more impediments to me getting out of here?

"Can't. I've got a family thing," I lied.

"Cool, no worries," he said and extended a fist to bump. "Bad calls tonight, but still a win, though."

I bumped his fist, nodded, hoisted my bag on my shoulder, and turned sharply to head for the exit. Security kept the back door clear of fans but getting out of the parking lot was fair game for anyone wanting an autograph. It didn't matter if you were a superstar captain like Xander or the rental here for a few months, everyone wanted players to stop, lean out their window, and sign merch. I signed what I could, smiled with the awkward selfies as people leaned toward my car, and even chatted to some of them about the car itself.

"You're the final Stanley Cup team signature I need," the last guy said, handing me a Washington jersey with my name and number. He looked kind of familiar, and I wondered if I'd met him before in the sea of faces waiting out here.

"Don't get caught carrying a Washington jersey around," I joked, and even though he smiled, he was a Washington fan and not a Rebels fan at all. Nothing wrong with that, but I was a Rebel now, and Washington was way back in my rearview mirror. "Who do I sign it to?"

"Verne," he muttered. "V.E.R.N.E." I wrote, and he kept talking. "I'm sorry you're playing here. They were wrong to let you go. You had some really terrible calls tonight, and you don't deserve them after winning the cup." His words ran on as if he'd rehearsed them all, and they spilled out in quick succession.

"Name of the game," I said, not really wanting to go down that particular rabbit hole with a fan after avoiding it with the journalists and Coach. "Night." I sketched a wave at Verne and cautiously pulled out of the parking lot and onto the main road, guiding my baby through the last of the exiting fans until, finally, I was on the 90 heading west out of town.

My apartment was in a small block of eight in Needham, far away from other hockey players and twenty miles from the city. I had the ground floor corner apartment, and the minute I shut the door behind me, I felt peace. Chloe always said I should use some of my money and go fancy, get a big place, somewhere in the center of the city, somewhere that made me feel I'd made it. Having money in the bank, creating college funds for my nieces, and hoarding everything until I retired was what I did— and spending wasn't on my to-do list. I had enough money to live the rest of my life the way I wanted to, maybe in hockey, maybe in a completely different area.

Maybe something with dogs.

I'd always loved dogs. I remembered one of the former players on the Railers had a dog sanctuary, and that intrigued me. Rentals like me, without a family, don't have dogs to cart around the country with them, but when I stopped moving, I was going to get four dogs. Big boisterous dogs that I could tussle with and love and come home to.

"Fuck." I dropped my bag to the floor, kicking it to the side so I didn't fall over it in the morning, and headed to the small kitchen, thinking about getting something to eat or drink. I was hungry, and I was tired, but most of all, with hockey responsibilities out of the way, in the privacy of my apartment…

…I was horny.

When I watched Webber skate away from me the moment I recognized him, all I could remember was how delicious were the sounds he made, and how much I'd had to hold back when I was fucking him. The way he begged, mewled, told me to go deep, not in words, but in the way he shifted. He'd let me fuck him so deep I thought I'd come on the spot. I'd been desperate to get him off before that happened. When I said I was going deeper, I heard the hitch in his voice, and I knew he was a long way over the edge.

I headed for the bathroom, all thoughts of a drink forgotten, and stared at myself in the mirror. Hard as iron, I pushed my hand into my pants, frantically loosening my belt, then shoved them and my underwear down until I could get my hands around my cock. I watched my eyes widen, my lips parted, and I scrambled for lube to slick my way. There was nothing delicate about how I was getting off. I used my other hand to pinch my balls, pulled my nipples, and through all of it, all I could think about was his face and the way he went limp in my arms after he came. I could imagine myself in him now, deep, thrusting, holding him still, not letting him move. A stranger in a bathroom.

Ropes of cum painted my mirror. I bent over the sink as my orgasm stole my breath. Regrets that I'd fucked Webber filled my head, though they were at war with the desperate urge to track him down and do it all over again.

Chapter Five

Webber

"SEVENTY-FIVE PITTSBURGH HAS A MINOR PENALTY." I made a slashing motion near my calf. "Two minutes for tripping." The hometown peeps were not happy. Many bad names floated down to me as I turned to find the Pittsburgh captain in my face.

"How was that tripping? Clearly, Lomac stepped on Kurt's stick."

"Come on, this is the NHL. You can stop," I teased and got an eye roll from the man. He was a good guy, most were, but they had to try their best for their teams. "Did that line ever work for you?"

"Once in peewee," he countered with a bit of humor. I chuckled and moved to my end of the ice for the next faceoff. "Maybe you should watch the replay," he called after me.

"Methinks we are seeing things differently, my man," I countered and got a wry smile from the men gathering for the puck drop. This was how it usually was for the most part. The players were respectful generally, teasing at times, making the game pleasant for those of us entrusted to keep the rules.

Things quieted down as the power play for Boston began. The faceoff was clean, with no infractions, and with a clean pass from the second-line center for Boston, the puck was in play. I quickly skated in reverse, my focus on the puck as it careened down the ice. Mike Mulligan was the other ref tonight, an older fellow about ready to retire. This was his final season, and I would miss him. He was a good ref. Even-tempered. The linesman whistled down an offside and another faceoff took place. It had been one of those games. Stops and starts galore.

I took a breather down by the Pittsburgh goalie, a pleasant man from Quebec who always had a quirky joke to tell the refs. I'd done my level best to avoid the Rebels as much as was feasible. It seemed the best way to ensure that Logan Mackie and I did not bump into each other. The few times our eyes had met, there had been a sizzle that snaked out between us like crackling fingers of static electricity. A rather annoying reaction to the man. It had been three weeks since that ill-fated hookup in Boston. Surely, that should've been enough time to purge the insane sexual attraction between us. Guess I was wrong. I had to think that, eventually, the attraction would burn out. Most do, or the majority of those I'd had over the years had, anyway.

Other than a few infractions for minor things, such as tripping or interference, the game was being played cleanly. Boston and Pittsburgh were both struggling to get points and stay in the top three slots of their respective divisions. When the third period began, one of the Rebels, the young Rowe lad, got a hair up his ass over something that was said by someone on the opposing team in front of the Pittsburgh net. The play had been called dead after the goalie had pinned the puck to the ice, and a few players had decided to chit-chat in the blue paint.

Rowe, who did not like to shove his face into other players' faces, was incensed. I stood there behind the net and watched as Rowe gave Larry March, a big Pittsburgh D-man, a punch in the face. Like out of the blue. Bang! It caught Larry off guard, but not enough to not fight back. As they say down in Satan's realm, all hell then broke loose. March shoved Rowe into the goalie, the goalie shoved Rowe, and through it all, I was blowing my whistle. Yeah, they never listen when their blood is up. Several other players arrived, all with Viking bloodlust in their eyes. I managed to get myself between Rowe and March, barking at everyone to calm the fuck down. Someone reached for Rowe and got my helmet instead.

One quick yank and it was off. I was furious, right then and there.

"Let the fuck go of me!" Rowe yelled as we jockeyed for control of his arms. March sounded off behind me. "I said let me go, you fucker!"

I'd been called that and worse by players. Water off a duck's back. If I got upset or hurt every time a hockey player called me a fucker, I'd be upset every damn game.

Austin Rowe—the chucklehead—opted to throw a punch at March but missed and clocked me on the cheek. Rowe's eyes rounded. Another big body arrived out of the ether, tugging March away and flinging him into the boards. With my arms around Rowe, who was now apologizing as if his life depended on it—and it might, because striking an official was serious shit—I spun to face whoever was adding to the chaos and stared right into Logan Mackie's terse face.

"You okay?" he asked amid the shouts, dirty words, and grunts of a near bench-clearing brawl.

"Fine. Get back out of this mess," I shouted, and he did, thankfully. March was now in the arms of Xander Holden, and they were not waltzing. I lost sight of Logan as I tried to keep Rowe from trying to reach March.

It took all four of the officials to break up the scrum. Players were yelling at each other as we marched them to their respective penalty boxes. It wasn't until we had the boxes filled with players that one of the linesmen pointed out that I had a cut on my cheek.

"Shit," I muttered, pulled out a hankie and dabbed at my face. It was bleeding, but not bad. "It's fine." I held the hankie to my face, intent on not leaving the game to get stitches. I've been clocked before during fights. And I will be clocked again, I was sure. "Let's get these penalties assessed."

It took a while. I skated over to the Rebels' bench to explain what was going to happen to Rowe, the head coach already making his case for his player as I arrived at the bench.

"Look, hey, look," I barked to be heard over the din of the crowd and several Rebels talking at me.

"That was not an intentional punch," Coach Franks was yelling. He was a big old defenseman who could bluster with the best of them. Great coach, beloved by his players, and loud as hell when he was arguing for his men.

"I know," I replied. "Oh, thank you." The head trainer called me closer to inspect my face. "Listen, no, listen. I know that was accidental. But the fact remains that he hit an official. Now…ouch." I winced as the trainer dabbed at the cut with some antiseptic. "There was no intent to harm, but he struck an official."

Boos rained down on me as more Pittsburgh players were sent to the sin bin. Both teams were getting equal time sitting on their asses in the penalty box. Well, aside from Rowe who was getting a longer rest.

"But it was an accident!" Franks roared, knowing that his young up-and-coming star was about to get some major time off.

"The point remains. He hit an official. That's an automatic misconduct, and he is out of this game. He'll probably have a hearing. I'd guess that he'll get a suspension and pay a fine. I'm sorry. Thank you." The head trainer gently placed a bandage on my cheek. The pain was a five on a scale of one to ten. I'd been hit in the face with a puck several years ago. Broke my cheekbone. Now that hurt badly. That was a plus twenty on the one to ten pain scale. "I know you know the rules. I'm sorry, this is now out of my hands."

The bench all began arguing young Rowe's cause. All except Logan who sat on the bench, eyes glued to me, as the Rebels fought for their teammate.

"I will speak on his behalf when the league calls me," I said, easing back from the bench to, hopefully, get this damn game restarted. Franks seemed mollified by that last comment. Rowe made his way to the locker room, looking like a whipped dog, and things resumed. By the end of the game, which went into overtime because why the hell not? I was seriously contemplating taking up sheep herding as an occupation. Boston had won in a shootout, which made the Pittsburgh fans mad. Thankfully, I was on my way home after this game. I had two days to rest before my next game in New York. I'd been happy with the medical attention from the head trainer, so I showered, changed, and made a beeline for the exit. All I wanted was a bed, some Advil, and a break from Logan Mackie's hungry looks.

I got as far as the corridor outside the away team's locker room and ran into Logan. He was fully dressed to leave, coat and hat, and a personal bag on his shoulder.

"Hey," he said as I skidded to a halt. He gave the hallway a fast look left then right, then leaned down close. Far too close. I could smell his spicy aftershave and it did things to my nether regions. Fucking A. What the hell kind of hold did this man have on me? "Are you okay?"

"Yeah, I'm fine. Thank you for your concern," I said loudly just in case someone was listening.

"Good, I was…well, good. Listen, about what happened with us—"

"This is not the place."

"But we need to talk. I can't stop thinking about it. What if someone finds out?"

"They will if you keep talking about it here." I threw another look around. Voices of men filled the halls, players in the locker room, trainers moving equipment, all the sounds of a team on the move. "Just pretend that it never happened."

He stared at me as if I had asked him to dance *Swan Lake*. "Can we please just talk?"

He seemed really distraught, which he had a right to be. I guess. I'd still not found much information on referees fraternizing with players—fraternizing, meaning a fast dicking in a bar bathroom while wearing Mardi Gras masks—so who knew what the blowout would be if it were found out? Brave new worlds.

"Fine, yes, we can talk. Not here. I have a room at the Silver Bridges Hotel. Room 242. Come to my room in an hour. We'll talk," I whispered, then drew back. He nodded, pulled his toque down over his brow, and made his way to the chartered bus waiting outside. I exhaled loudly, darting looks this way and that as I called for a ride.

The trip to the hotel was a quiet one. I was not in the mood to chat with the driver, so I paid and tipped, and then, hustled my ass into the lobby, avoiding talking to anyone. Not that people knew me. I wasn't a famous athlete. Some people who knew hockey might know who I was, but out of the stripes it was doubtful. And that was how we officials preferred it.

I rode up to the second floor alone, lost in my thoughts. The key card pinged softly when I scanned it, and I entered my room. It was quite nice. They all are. But they're all rented rooms. I missed my little home in Long Branch, New Jersey. It was a small house, nothing fancy, but it suited me well. The town was near the beach and was proudly happy to tell the world that it was the birthplace of Bruce Springsteen, whom I enjoyed tremendously. In the summer, I could walk on the beach and go deep sea fishing. Also, it was close enough to several NHL cities so that I could get to games expediently

I'd just gotten my shoes off and removed my coat when a soft tap-tap-tap sounded at the door. Wow, he must have broken land speed records to get here. I yanked open the door and there Logan stood, his toque in his hand, looking like a dog someone had left beside the road.

"Come in," I softly said, opening the door for him. He moved past me, the rich smell of his aftershave tickling my nose. "Do you want something to drink?"

"No, no, I shouldn't." He gave the room a fast perusal. "Nice room."

"It's quite nice. The patio looks out at the Monongahela." I moved closer, ignoring the tightening in my loins as I drew nearer. "I can take your coat."

He turned from the view to look at me.

"So, tonight's game was something weird," he remarked as he shrugged out of his coat. "You know Austin—"

I held up a hand to stall him. "If you're here to plead your teammate's case then you can keep your coat on and go back to your hotel. The call was made. I stand by it. The league will decide the rest. As I told Franks, I will give my side of the story, if and when I'm called. I don't think it was intentional, but he was pretty damn mad at me as well, so I'm leaving the final call to the league." He blinked at me.

"Oh, well, yeah, I get that and agree. No, I'm not here to try to make you change your mind or anything." He ran a big hand over his hair, making it stand up at wonky angles. "I was just concerned."

"Concerned about what?" He passed me his coat. I laid it over the back of a padded chair, my sight never leaving his.

"You. Your face." His hand rose slowly as if he were trying to touch a wild stallion. With great hesitance, he ran the tips of his fingers over the bandage on my cheek. The touch was so light, I barely felt it on my face, but Lord above, did I feel it everywhere else. "Your face is too pretty to be marred up like mine."

All rational thought fled as my dick grew hard. The big doofus thought I was pretty. Shit. How did I respond to this tenderness? I certainly couldn't just blather on about how we needed to keep a distance and act responsibly to avoid any hint of scandal. My eyes widened slightly as his fingertips skimmed down to cup my jaw, then my lashes grew heavy.

"I have nuts," I whispered as he stroked my throat.

"I know," he replied. "I've seen them."

"No, salted nuts in the snack drawer."

"Oh." Something flared to life in his eyes. He breathed in deeply, his nostrils flaring, and my toes curled into the carpeting. The air came alive around us, sparks of desire riding the dry currents, snapping, and dancing as they pirouetted around us. You could taste lust in the air.

He never said another damn word. He just reached for me. And I went. Like metal shavings to a magnet. His mouth crashed down over mine, teeth clacking, as my hands dove under his clothes to find his ass. I took both meaty cheeks in hand and squeezed. Hard. Logan moved me around the room as if I were a mere wisp of a man, which I was not. I had played hockey, I worked out, and I was no featherweight. His ability to put me where he wanted me was fucking hot. Apparently, he wanted me in the bathroom. It wasn't a big room by any means, but there was a counter which he rammed me against, his hands cupping my face as his tongue roamed over my teeth and the roof of my mouth.

Since my hands were free, I got to work on our pants, fumbling with zippers until his cock and mine were free.

"Turn around," he grunted when the kiss broke. I did as he commanded, lying my belly on the cold counter, giving him my ass with no second thoughts. That would come later. "Fuck, I love seeing you in this position with your eyes all dark and your tight ass ready for my cock."

"Yes, so ready," I panted, watching him in the mirror above the sink. The lights in the bathroom were off, but the illumination from the desk lamp in the suite was enough. "Stuff…in the bag." I grabbed a neatly rolled hand towel for myself. Logan gave my ass cheek a pat, rummaged in my shaving kit, and found the small tube of lube and a sleeve of condoms.

"Always so prepared, you zebras," he tossed out as he booted up, then smeared lube over my ass. And I mean all over my ass. Not just my hole. "Thought I might find a whistle in there."

"I keep that…beside the bed…oh hell," I gasped as his fingers pressed into me. Eyes fluttering shut, I bowed my head as he worked me open. A low moan of disappointment burbled out of me when he removed those fat digits. My displeasure only lasted for a second because his prick slid right in to fill the void and then some. "Fuck," I hissed as the burning pleasure sent flickers of lust through me. I backed up, eager for more, and Logan growled like a panther.

"Greedy man," he rasped, then thrust, driving that massive cock into me. I think I may have had an out-of-body experience for a moment—it was that fucking good. Logan began pounding away, his balls slapping mine, as I threw a hand up to keep my head from slamming into the mirror. Logan threaded his fingers into my hair, pulling me back and up so he could feast on my neck and mouth as he rocked in and out. I licked at his mouth wantonly, reaching back to find his round ass. Muscles rolled under my hand as he pumped away. He bit down on my shoulder when he came, making me cry out in pleasure. His hand found my cock, gave it a rough tug or two, and I blew apart, coating the counter with cum. So much for using that hand towel to catch the mess.

Words were pointless things, so I didn't bother to use any as my body convulsed madly. He milked me dry, his mouth still on my shoulder, sucking gently like a sated vampire. Each pulse of his cock inside me made me quiver in his arms.

"Fuck, you're pretty," he moaned into my flesh, his fingers smearing spunk over my cock before coming up to wipe my spend on my lips. I licked it off. He made a feral sound, then spun me to face him, his cock sliding out to leave a slippery trail over my hip and belly. He kissed me hungrily, lapping at my mouth and lips before applying more warm cum to my lips. Over and over, he did this, our tongues rolling over the other as we licked and lapped like dogs cleaning a bowl of beef broth.

"Holy hell," I panted, letting my brow fall to his shoulder. He still had his dress shirt and suit jacket on. I was still mostly fully dressed as well. He nuzzled at the base of my neck. I breathed in his scent, held it in my lungs, and then, let it slowly out through my nose.

"So that happened again," he softly said while fondling my ass, his fingers gliding over my cheek to find my tender hole. I mewled like a kitten full of milk. Then, what he'd said sank in, which, thankfully, took place before his fingers could sink into me one more time, because fuck knows if that happened I'd be heels to Jesus again.

I rested my forehead on his shoulder. "What the hell is wrong with us? We know this is going to go wrong. Why do we keep fucking?!"

Chapter Six

Logan

WHY DO WE KEEP FUCKING?

Hell, I didn't know how to answer that. I could be super honest and admit that Webber was the sexiest thing I'd ever laid eyes on and that the experience in the bathroom—both of them—was some of the hottest sex I'd ever had, but I'm not sure that was what he was looking for. Or I could think of something clever about traveling, being a hockey player, having sex with a random stranger, any port in a storm…hell, I didn't know what to say. So, as he eased himself away from me, I settled for a shrug.

"That's not helpful." Webber sounded tired. "Not helpful at all."

"I don't know what you want me to say." I sounded just as tired. "I came here because we need to talk, but fuck…" I carded my hands through my hair and gripped tight. Already the endorphins had subsided, and I felt as if I'd messed up something vitally important.

Webber cleared his throat. "Okay, let's be serious for a minute. It's important that this is consensual and that we acknowledge it is."

"I would never force myself on someone, you—"

"Not that kind of consensual, idiot," Webber interrupted. "I mean, you accept that I'm not using my authority and power over you to force you to do something you didn't want and that you didn't...um...do the thing with me."

"Fuck you?" I teased at his rambling, and he winced.

"Yeah, that. It's important for you to know you won't gain any advantage on the ice just by doing...that."

"Anyway, back to you having power over *me*." I tried to lighten the conversation, but he was so serious, and to be honest, he *did* have power over me, and a magic about him that made me want to sink inside him and lose my mind.

"Stop smiling. This is serious. People might think I forced you to do this."

"That's not right. We've done this to each other. I wasn't here looking for an advantage," I added.

"If people found out we'd done this, twice..."

"Shit, is there a rule?" I asked.

"Not that I can see, but there *are* issues of common sense. The NHL will draw the line at zero as the best way to avert any issues. Coaches, players, fans, and media can be paranoid enough, or jaded, to believe anything more than a handshake is proof of collusion between skaters and refs. You asking me if I'm okay after Austin hit me or following me down a corridor is going to look bad for both of us."

"Okay—"

"So, we're not doing this again," Webber concluded, and I nodded mutely. He was right. If people thought for one moment that either of us was trying to gain from having sex, then the headlines wouldn't be pretty. We both had too much riding on this, not least our reputations.

I desperately wanted to argue something that meant we could carry on, but seriously, I had nothing, and what had happened here tonight tasted like ashes. Resigned, I headed for the door, glancing back just once to see Webber leaning against the bathroom door. He had his arms crossed over his chest and was resolute. We weren't doing this again, and the decision was based on thoughtful consideration for both our jobs, and not at all based on the insanity of lust that had taken us this far.

"Fucking you was amazing," I said as I gripped the door handle.

"Getting fucked by you was amazing," he replied.

And before I could go back and do something stupid, I left, because I had to be okay with the decision. *I* am *okay*. So why, in the elevator heading down, did I feel bereft? I'd never been with anybody so completely fuckable, someone who had hockey in common with me, who understood the stresses and strains of being on the road. Why did I have to give it all up with someone that might just be the perfect person for me?

Fuck it all to hell and back.

WE WERE ONLY FIVE GAMES FROM THE END OF THE SEASON now, and it had become mathematically inevitable that we were going to meet the Railers in the first round of the race for the Cup, which is why Coach had us in the conference room with the big screen on our off day.

"…so, it's the only way in. And I want to see some positive action from the right wing at all times in the lines going up against Ten."

"Need a fucking miracle," someone murmured from behind me. I hoped to god that Coach hadn't heard whoever it was because I hated the way people spoke about the big names with such feelings of inevitability— almost as if we'd lost already. Yes, Tennant Rowe was near impossible to defend against, but not *completely* impossible. He might be a superstar or a guaranteed future Hall of Famer, but he has his weak spots. Some of those were rooted in the two people on his wing and some were the fact that I felt his play was sometimes predictable.

"Coach, can I just say something?" Boston was the team who wanted their players to have input, but this was the first time I'd raised my head above the parapet.

"As long as it's not that we need a fucking miracle," Coach said with a pointed glance at someone a few rows behind me. "Tennant Rowe is *not* invincible."

Not one person in the room added a single thing: no cursing, no grumbling, and certainly, no snorts of disbelief.

I took a moment to get my thoughts in order, and Coach waited patiently. "I like a lot about the way Rowe plays—he's *too* fast, *too* accurate, and looking at his stats in isolation, he appears almost untouchable."

Coach muttered something under his breath. "He's not untouchable," he said.

I glanced over at Austin, who inclined his head in agreement. It must be hard for him to sit here in a meeting and hear us dissect his cousin's game. The Rowe family were incredibly close, cousins included, and I'd seen Tennant cross over to Austin after a game and tap helmets, acknowledging that they were family, on and off the ice. Thing is, Boston as a team wasn't here to respect family boundaries or to make allowances. Austin was fiercely protective of his cousin off the ice, but when he was skating as part of the team, his passion to win for Boston was everything. Take the fact that he was due for his player safety meeting in a few hours for letting his passion rule his head. Something had made him snap, and maybe all of us in the room had an instinct for what it might be— the ice wasn't a place where everybody was super polite. Some teams, or rather some players, would use everything at their disposal to mess with the opposite teams' heads.

"Agreed that Ten isn't untouchable. What he does, though, is that he adjusts on the fly to the way the other team plays. It's subtle, but it's there. Like when he went up against Washington last week. I mean, they play a very physical game, maybe *too* physical, and part of what they did was to attempt to take Rowe out of the game. When you watch the game film, you can see how he adjusts his skating based on that targeted attack—he's faster out of the corners, his head is up every single moment, and he darts quickly so that he doesn't get trapped."

Coach nodded thoughtfully. "Go on."

"Well, throughout the attacks, he uses speed to get to

the puck first, and his hockey sense is so insane that the Washington guys just ended up face-planting into the plexiglass. So then, they focused on the wingmen, probably thinking that without his wingmen, Ten might be less of an issue. And all he did was adjust his game again, this time to protect the guys he was with. I mean, this is nothing new. We all do that. Adjust our game, I mean." There was a murmur of agreement. "But if we can rotate what we are doing much faster, even from shift to shift, crowd him one time, work cleanly on separating him from his wingmen in the other, we could throw his game off balance. He can cycle rapidly through changing his game, so we should as well. Also…"

"There's more?" Someone chuckled from behind me. Probably the same person who thought Rowe was untouchable. I could feel the embarrassment building inside me, not used to doing this, putting myself front and center and open to criticism. But I knew I was making sense.

"Shut your mouth, Perrin, and you might learn something after all your fuckups last game."

Silence. And then someone—Perrin, one of the guys up from our AHL team—cleared his throat. "Sorry, Coach."

"Rowe is focused and purposeful," I continued. "But he's one part of a big team, and remember, the Railers are still behind us in rankings."

Coach nodded his agreement, but he stood there silently for a moment as he considered what I'd said. "Good. That's the thinking I want here. Does anybody have anything else to add to that? Thoughts?"

The meeting carried on for another hour and when we left, a few of the players fist-bumped me, including Perrin, and I assumed it was their way of saying they appreciated I'd spoken up, or even that maybe I'd made sense. I felt like I'd actually made a positive step forward with the team, but never expected Austin to follow me to the kitchen.

"Can we talk?" Austin closed the door behind us, glancing through a little inset window to see if anyone else was out there.

"Of course, I'm sorry if I offended you for talking about Ten."

Austin seemed confused for a moment, blinking at me, and then he shook his head. "No, God, not at all. We're family, and that is more than everything *when* we are not on the ice. Do you think Jamie is down there in Florida not dissecting Ten's play or mine, maybe? Not that I've done anything admirable recently." He sighed heavily as if the weight of the world was on his shoulders. "That's not why I wanted to talk to you."

"What's up?" I busied myself by making coffee in a to-go cup to take home. The arena kitchen had all the best stuff, way more than my small kitchen had, and it had become something of a ritual to enjoy the journey with some extra caffeine. That and Queen's greatest hits on repeat was all I needed to chill.

"Marquis said he saw you talking to Webber." I stiffened with my back to him and had to pretend very hard that it was vital to measure out the correct creamer. "Said that you caught him in the corridor." Relief flooded me until I thought which corridor? This is why doing things that are wrong, even if they feel right—and boy did sex with Webber feel right—can come back and bite you in the ass.

"After the game?" I qualified quickly, wanting to put this conversation to a stop if he was going anywhere near me being in a corridor in a hotel with a referee who I shouldn't be anywhere near. I don't remember seeing Marquis there, but was I really conscious of anything that night apart from thinking about how fast I could get up to the room?

"Ref Webber told Coach he'd put in a good word for me at the player hearing, but did he say anything to you? Did you ask him if he was okay? How badly did I hurt him? I can't believe I did that." Austin slumped to the nearest seat and scrubbed his eyes. So much for me leaving the arena with a nice hot coffee. Austin clearly needed somebody to talk to, and maybe that would have to be me. I made a second coffee and placed it on the table in front of him, then took the seat opposite. Austin's worries had fallen out in a tumble of words, and now I needed to pick my way through them.

"First, I just asked him if he was okay. It was just a general question." Stop talking. He didn't need to know that. He frowned at me.

"Sure, of course."

"He knew it was an accident, what happened. He said the same thing to me about putting in a good word, and also told me that nothing I could say would influence what he was going to report."

"Shit. Did he think that you'd gone up to him to convince him otherwise? I don't need that, I promise. I did what I did—I fucked up—and I need to pay the piper, but I don't need any favors."

He was working himself up into anger, but it wasn't me he was angry with, and he seemed to realize that at the same moment I was going to call him on it.

"Shit, I'm sorry," he blurted. "I just don't know what happened with March. I've had worse stuff said to me, but…"

"But what? What exactly did March say to you?"

He dipped his gaze to the table, cradling his mug, and sighed. Everyone expected so much from Austin, that he'd be the new Ten, that he'd follow in Brady's footsteps, that he'd be as good as his cousin Jamie. But he was just this kid who was very good at hockey. The weight of the Rowe name had to be a heavy burden, but he handled it really well. Well, apart from when he didn't.

"At first it was nothing I haven't heard before, you know, the gay stuff about me. Then, it was about Ten, but then, they went on attack about Jared and Ten's kids, and I won't have that." He raised his gaze to meet mine, his eyes shining with emotion, and my chest was tight with compassion. It was bad enough that there were still homophobic slurs being used in a league where teams had queer representation. But the worst thing anyone can throw at a hockey player is shade about family. "I'm not going into specifics, not until I've spoken to player safety, but I swear, if I heard that shit again, I'd react exactly the same way. I'd want to kill them." He subsided. "But I'm sorry, and I know it's put the team in a really dangerous position."

"Listen, kid," I began as if being a few weeks short of

my thirty-first birthday meant I was that much more experienced than Austin, who wasn't long into his twenties.

"Yeah?" he prompted when I paused, his tone cautious.

"No, I shouldn't call you that. You're not a kid. You're a grown man who feels things deeply, and who gives everything to the sport he loves, and his family, and that makes you the best kind of person. When you speak to player safety, you tell them every single word that was thrown at you. Be as honest as you can; don't apologize for the love you have inside you for your family. Don't let them make less of what you feel. Okay?"

I know I was appearing intense, but nobody in this league had the right to question a man's love or loyalty or expect them to change how they feel. Player safety had the job of making sure that players and all the officials stayed safe, but they needed to listen to the skaters involved. March should get an interview as well, demanding to know why he'd even considered voicing the vile poison he'd spilled in front of Austin. Maybe he would if Austin was completely honest.

It was only after Austin fist-bumped me and headed out to his video link interview that I realized maybe my advice was colored by my exasperation that I couldn't call up Webber and take him out for a steak dinner, and then, fuck him over the bed in the closest hotel.

I made it home just after six, after checking that Coach was hanging around to be with Austin after his hearing. Actually, it wasn't just Coach, but half the damn team, all of whom sat in the locker room, joking, and laughing, and not one admitting how worried they were. It wasn't about the fact that Austin was likely to miss a game, and it wasn't as if he couldn't afford a fine. It was about the fact that something had triggered Austin, and that it had to have been bad. I considered sitting with them, but I felt wrong, as if my skin was too tight, and I really needed my space.

Still, not even Queen helped me stop thinking about Webber and the sex and the big no that was our fucking. By the time I stepped inside my place, my head was a mess, and my libido was all over the place. When there was a current absence of sex and no possibility of sex with the hottest man I'd ever fucked on the horizon, I couldn't keep my thoughts straight. We hadn't exchanged numbers —people didn't do that for hookups. Anyway, me having a referee's number on my phone...yeah, not happening.

Only, imagine if we had exchanged numbers, we could be having really hot and nasty phone sex.

I just wish my right hand was enough to replace what I wanted right now.

Webber was an addiction.

OUR NEXT GAME, AWAY IN NEW JERSEY, WAS A SHIT SHOW.

Austin was out serving a three-game suspension, and as if the fates had intervened to make things worse, Webber was officiating the game. Of course, every single question before the game was about Webber and Austin. Some suggested that Austin had gotten away with too much by only having three lost games with a twenty-thousand-dollar fine. While others suggested that Webber would now be biased against Boston. It was all white noise. It was also an enormous distraction to the team, and mostly to me. I couldn't switch off from seeing Webber or hearing Webber. Practically fucking dying every time he made a call in that sexy as fuck tone, with all his hand movements, and his frowning, and his grin as he chatted with the other officials.

I'd seen nothing in my life as perfectly sexy as Webber. It might only be just sex, but the thought of being inside him, this time slowing down, going to my knees and—

"Wake the fuck up, Lomac!" Coach Franks yelled as I lost yet another battle for the puck right near the bench. By the time I'd recognized it was me fucking up, the game had already moved down the other end of the ice. My inattention had gotten me split from the rest of my line, ending up in the ass end of nowhere, completely messed up. *Fuck.* Thankfully, the puck ended up coming my way. I corralled it and got back in the game enough so that we didn't end up having yet another goal against us. When we finished, a loss of four goals to our measly zero, a screaming crowd of New Jersey fans let us know exactly how happy they were. I was done.

Clearly, I can't think straight when Webber is on the ice, and I needed to sort this out, sooner rather than later.

Chapter Seven

Webber

THE INCOMPARABLE JOHN LITHGOW ONCE SAID SOMETHING about musicals sending you out of the theater filled with music.

Which was totally true and right now, after calling another game where I had to pretend Logan Mackie was just a random player who had not fucked me into another dimension, I was ready for some music in my soul. Yes, I love musicals. And at the top of those beloved musicals is anything *Fosse*. So being in desperate need of a lift, I headed out after the game to a small little theater located just around the corner from my home. My neighborhood, only a few miles from the New Jersey pro teams' arena, but in a different world than the city, was all kinds of bohemian, and I just adored it. There were yoga studios, meditation centers, play centers, farm markets, health food stores, and vegan eateries out the yin-yang. Everyone accepted everyone else. It was a kind of nirvana, to be honest, and the perfect place for a queer man with a stressful job to de-stress.

I'd visited this small quirky theater numerous times, and with a quick check of the times online, was thrilled to discover that they were doing a *Fosse* month with midnight showings. Jumping into my car, I hightailed to the theater, eager to find a seat, eat stale popcorn, and let whatever gem was playing tonight take me the hell away for two hours. The streets were wet from a small shower that had moved past during the game, the marquee above the theater reflecting green, red, and blue on the road. I nearly squealed in joy when I saw *Cabaret* was the midnight show this week. Ugh, I adored Liza Minelli and Joel Grey. Michael York was nothing to sneeze at either. Giddy with excitement, I pulled around back, parked in the nearly empty lot, and jogged round front, my sneakers splashing in several small puddles. I pulled in a deep breath of rain fresh air, smiled, and pulled open the old doors, inhaling the smell of popped corn.

"Perfection," I whispered as I gave the nearly empty lobby a quick once over. The place was an old, delightful thirties movie house, glitzy and lovingly tended. There was only one screen, so they juggled more contemporary films with the old classics—the newer movies playing at the popular times and the older films getting the midnight runs. I paid the young man at the ticket counter, bought some popcorn—even though I knew it was from the earlier shows—and got a small root beer. Happy as a lark with my goodies and the knowledge that I'd be lost in *Fosse* goodness soon, I turned my head when the front door creaked open. My straw flitted from my hand to the dark red carpet when Logan walked through the heavy wooden doors. His gaze met mine. I gaped. He gaped. His eyebrows climbed to his hairline. And there he stood, staring as if he wasn't sure if he should proceed or not.

"I can go," he called up to me. I shook my head. "You sure?"

"You do know that *Cabaret* is playing here, right?" I had to ask. Maybe he had misread the theater's website time listings. "It's a musical."

"Yeah."

I shot a glance at the kid at the snack counter. He was deeply interested in what was taking place with Logan and me.

"Okay then, buy your ticket," I replied with as little emotion as I could muster. Talk about hard to pull off. My belly had turned somersaults when I'd spied him. Whatever this thing was we had going, I really needed to get control of it.

Bending down to pick up my straw, I tossed it into the overflowing trash can by the napkin and straw stand and grabbed another before heading into the theater. I took a seat in the last row on the left. There were two other people here, way down front, making out by the looks. I settled into my seat. It wasn't too comfortable. It was an old movie theater seat, not one of those plush reclining things that vibrated and fed you grapes like they have at the cineplex at the mall. This theater was all about the old-time experience of a grand movie palace, just on a small scale. So, what if your tailbone ached by the end of the show? Velveteen wallpaper, scalloped gold borders along the wall and ceiling, and glass wall sconces that threw muted light surrounded you. Try to find that kind of ambiance in a forty screen megaplex.

I sank down into my seat, shrugged off my coat, and placed my soda into the cup holder on my right. Logan entered. I pretended to be sorting through kernels, but was, in fact, peeking at the man. He was far too good-looking to not admire.

"Oh seriously?" I mumbled, kind of miffed, yet kind of glad, when he strode over and sat down beside me. I threw him a dark look. "There are a hundred other seats in this theater, and you have to plunk your bubble butt here?" I waved a piece of popcorn at him, then threw it into my mouth, chewing aggressively.

"I hate going to the movies alone," he confessed, wiggling his wide shoulders so that his left arm was pressing into my right arm.

"I don't mind at all," I countered, staring at the dancing candy bars on the screen. They even played old-time concession stand cartoons before the midnight shows. "I enjoy being alone." That was kind of a lie, but it sounded tough.

He shrugged, reached into his tub of popcorn, then shoved a handful into his mouth. I stared in a mixture of shock and admiration. Impressive. I bet he could fit a big, fat—

"You do know that this is a musical, right?" I asked again because my mind was not allowed to go down that dirty little path.

"You asked me that already," he replied around more popcorn in his mouth. The man was probably starving. He'd played a rough, physical game. I was always hungry after my time on the ice as well. Probably movie theater popcorn and candy bars weren't ideal for either of us, but I needed this respite to get away from…him.

"I know I did, but I just can't picture a hockey player watching a musical," I admitted and plucked a kernel from my tub.

"You're a hockey player."

Damn. Okay, yes, I was. Or had been. "Not anymore, but I get your point." He flashed me a quick smile, his lips all coated with butter. It took all my willpower to stay in my seat. The man wore slippery lips really well. "How did you ever get into musicals?"

"I dated a theater major in college."

"Ah, okay." I glanced down at the make-out couple. Jeez. They were really going at it.

"What about you?"

"My mother was a singer in her youth and always dreamed of being on Broadway, so she dragged my twin brother and me to every play within a hundred miles of our hometown. After marrying my dad and having two boys in one fell swoop, her dreams of being on stage kind of evaporated."

"That's too bad. Maybe she can find a theater group near where she lives. Where is that?"

"Ontario, and she has. She likes to joke that she's got grease paint in her blood." I chuckled, and so did Logan. "The person who you dated in college…were they someone special?"

"Yeah, she was really nice. Great dancer. Legs that went on for miles."

A little flare of something I didn't want to acknowledge poked at me. "Do you keep in touch with this special lady?" I knew next to nothing about him. Shit, he could even be married, although I hadn't seen a ring. Please do not let him be married...

"Not anymore. Since the divorce, we've kind of drifted apart. She's remarried now, with a new baby."

"Oh, well, I'm sorry about your marriage," I softly said as I plucked another piece of popcorn out of the bright yellow tub.

"It's okay. Traveling and moving all the time is killer on relationships."

"Yes. Yes, it really is." I knew that firsthand. Most people wanted stability and a partner that was home every night. Hell, *I* wanted that. But my job wanted other things from me. Like being in a new city almost every other night. I glanced to the side. He didn't look too upset with our conversation. That was good. I didn't want to upset him. I much preferred seeing him smile or bantering back and forth with him. "Have you seen this film before?"

"Mm, no." He wiped his lips with a crumpled napkin. Oh, to be a napkin... "I did see it once on stage when I was in college. My girlfriend—who became my wife—had the role that Liza Minelli has in the film. She was pretty good."

"Not as good as Liza, I'm sure."

That made him laugh. It was a rough burst of mirth that made me smile. That was a sound that I could enjoy hearing more.

"Well, who is? Aside from her mother," he replied.

"True, true."

The lights dimmed, but the couple down front didn't seem to notice. I wiggled around in my seat, my tailbone already complaining, and stared up at the big screen. Logan gave me a nudge in the side and pointed down at the front row. The couple had disappeared.

"They just hit the floor," he whispered in my ear, his breath buttery sweet.

"They'll have Jujubes stuck to their ass," I said in a sotto voce aside. He roared with laughter, which brought one head up from the floor to check things out. We both sunk down into our seats, snickering like teenagers until the person returned to his or her lover.

I kept sneaking a peek at Logan. Through "Willkommen" and "Maybe This Time," and even "Cabaret" itself, I couldn't keep my eyes on the screen. Logan was thoroughly enjoying the songs and story, and even the romance between Sally and her language professor. He would whisper things to me here and there, but for the most part, he was silent, smiling at the screen, and utterly charming. This was not helping me to boot the attraction that I was feeling for him at all. It would have been much better had he scoffed at hearing what the film was, or chided me for being such a typical gay, or even called me a pansy for liking musicals. No. The big, gorgeous hunk had to be all sorts of into musical theater. How on earth was I supposed to pry him out of my mind if he liked Liza Minelli?

When the closing credits rolled, the wall sconces brightened. The couple down front stood, righted their clothes, and marched up the aisle as if they'd not just fucked in public. The man gave us a wink as he held his lady's hand.

"Well, that was two shows for the price of one ticket," I tossed out as I rose and pulled on my jacket.

"Shame we couldn't see more of the free show," Logan tossed out, taking my empty soda cup and popcorn tub, and carrying them to the trash can just inside the door.

"Do you watch a lot of porn?" I enquired while we made our way outside. The night was deep now, traffic light. The puddles were still present, but the black top was drier. The late April air had a slight nip to it.

"No more than anyone else." He stood on the sidewalk, glancing this way and that. I joined him, stepping out from under the marquee just as the door behind us locked.

"Are you still hungry?" I asked, although I knew I shouldn't.

"Nah, not really. The jumbo popcorn and four boxes of Butterfinger bites took the edge off," he said as he turned to face me. The glow from the marquee threw shadows over his rugged face. Such a handsome face. Masculine, strong. "I'll have to ride a stationary bike for ten miles tomorrow morning to work all that junk off."

"I feel that." I patted my belly and glanced off in the direction of my car. "I'm parked around back. Would you like a ride to your hotel?"

"No, it's okay. I already have a ride on the way."

"Good, good." Ugh, this was awkward. "I had a nice time tonight."

"Yeah, me too. Nice to know we like other things about each other than mere fucking."

"Is what we do mere fucking?" I teased, unsure of why I was engaging in this kind of back and forth at all. It was super close to flirting.

"No, there's nothing mere about us."

Wow. I just...*wow*. That rocked my world. Who knew six words could be so powerful? And so damn true. No matter how hard I'd been trying to purge Logan from my head the past month or so, he was still there, smiling that shy smile of his, pulling me closer with his love of *Fosse*.

I didn't have the balls to reply earnestly, so I said nothing at all. *Should I invite him home to my place?*

"So, listen, there's nothing to stop us from getting a coffee when you're calling the next Boston game, right?"

I blinked away the image of him in my tidy bedroom and focused back on the invitation, shoving my hands into my jacket pockets before I cradled his face and kissed him into a stupor.

"Is coffee a euphemism for fucking me in the bathroom again?"

He chortled, but there was a fire in those blue eyes of his that was impossible to deny.

"No, coffee is just coffee. A ref and a player can just be friends, can't they?" He held out his hand. I stared at it for a long moment, then placed my cell in his palm. He entered his number and passed it back. I did the same for him. All kinds of warning klaxons fired off, but there were no rules about texting a friend for coffee. Right?

"Are we truly ever going to be just friends?" I asked, and the question hung there in the late-night air. His ride pulled up, but he'd not yet answered. Maybe, I shouldn't have asked. Probably shouldn't have asked.

"Probably not," he finally said and gave my fingers a fast squeeze before opening the back door of the dark blue sedan and riding away.

"Well, damn it." I sighed, my gaze on those taillights until they disappeared from sight.

TWO WEEKS LATER, I WAS BACK IN BOSTON.

I received an invitation to referee the first round of the eastern divisional semi-finals. It is quite interesting how they pick the refs. The NHL vice president and head of officiating picks twenty refs and twenty linesmen from a pool of all available officials. The league then matches up the pairs by personality, experience, energy, and style. They notify us by email that we were picked, and then, we must wait until the matchups are finalized. Refs switch out every game, so I'd be here in Boston tonight, then, I was off to New York to Pittsburgh, and then, a trip to Buffalo, and so on and so on.

We'd all sat in on a mass conference call yesterday with the head of officiating for a long talk about consistency, ensuring there was good communication, and getting a fast hand when a game gets messy early. I was calling the Railers vs. Rebels game one, so I didn't foresee there being too much in the way of dirty play. Both teams were well-coached and known for their clean hits. We touched on other aspects of game play, and then, they congratulated us for making the cut. I'll admit to being proud that I'd been chosen.

My father was ecstatic when I'd called home to let them know.

"Make sure you let them know early who's in charge," Dad told me while Mom was singing something from *Fiddler on the Roof* in the background. She was practicing for a summer run at the local theater in town.

"I'm not expecting too much trouble," I informed him. Things were different in the game now than they were when he'd been officiating. He'd had the pleasure of calling a few playoff games in Philly back in the '70s. He'd just been given his whistle—no fancy schemes for training or anything like that. Talk about indoctrination by fire. "This is a different league than when you were calling things."

"Yeah, I know, but tempers rise when the Cup is on the line. Call things tight, Webber. Show them right off that they're not going to get away with bullshit."

I thanked him for the advice, told him to kiss Mom for me, and was distracted when my cell buzzed with a text from Logan.

How do you find a zebra?

I snorted. Great, now we were sharing zebra jokes.

I don't know. How?

Look under ze-shirt.

Ugh.

I have tons more. If you meet me for coffee, I'll tell you some.

How about we meet for coffee, and you don't tell me some?

Killjoy. Perfect. See you tomorrow.

I LEFT MY HOTEL ROOM FEELING A BUZZ IN MY VEINS. Playoff hockey was always exciting. It just felt different. The air was more charged. The fans were louder. Also, this was totally not a good thing, but I was excited to see Logan. Somehow, he'd talked me into coffee while I was in town. Yes, we'd started texting each other after that movie date. Logan was damn funny in his gruff way.

We have a coffee date tomorrow morning before I have to leave for Manhattan for the New York vs. Pittsburgh series. It felt kind of daring to me to simply sit down in public and have coffee. I was waffling terribly about the whole thing. Perhaps, I should call Dan Hamilton, the head of officiating, and ask a few carefully worded questions about friendships with players. I suspected I knew what his reply would be, especially during the playoffs.

I sighed as I laced up my skates. Logan and I were walking a very fine wire here. And by wire, I meant thread. Maybe even coffee was a bad idea. But fuck, I wanted to spend some time with the man. Even an hour over a bagel would be enough to carry me through until…

Until what? Where do you think this is going to go?

That was the big question, wasn't it? This thing of ours really couldn't go anywhere. Not with him playing and me officiating. And yet, here I was trying to decide what kind of bagel I'd order when we snuck off to be together.

"Webber, you ready, buddy?" I glanced up to see Pierre Blanchet smiling at me from the door of the officials' room. Pierre was older than me, well-liked by the players and coaches, and a stickler for keeping sticks on the ice.

We'd be seeing a lot of stick infractions tonight. Which wasn't a bad thing, as long as we also just let the boys play. He and I had worked together numerous times, and I admired him greatly.

"I'm ready," I replied, then slid my pea-less whistle onto my finger. "Let's go do this hockey thing."

Chapter Eight

Logan

FIRST GAME OF THE FIRST ROUND FOR THE RACE TO THE Stanley Cup against the Railers, and we were tied at two goals each—so evenly matched that any advantage achieved by us was immediately snatched back. Likewise, every mistake we made, the Railers seemed to duplicate. There was no room for either team to pull ahead, and even though we agreed to try switching up a strategy against their top line, any advantage didn't appear to last long. There wasn't much any team could do when faced with someone like Tennant Rowe on a good night, a man who seemed to pull a slap shot out of nowhere, and as was usual for him, he was making our defensive pairings work hard.

On the plus side, we had our very own Rowe, and Austin was playing as if this was game seven, and not just game one. At first, it worried me that he was putting himself in too many bad spots, trying to create the magic, but like his cousin, he was slippery quick, and we actually had two teams that were playing the best hockey of their lives right now. Given we'd won our second place in the division, with the Railers a few points behind us, it meant we had home advantage for the first two games. No one can deny that home advantage is a very real positive. From the moment players park their cars, right on through to the capacity crowd with a vast percentage chanting our names, I swear it gives the home team an extra boost.

And this was exactly what Coach Franks was telling us in the fifteen minutes before the final period. The mood in the locker room was upbeat. No one looked pissed, although Xander was staring down at a tablet, watching the Railers' second goal, and frowning. He wouldn't be looking for where an individual, or the team, had made mistakes, but at how we could stop the same thing from happening again—that's what made him an excellent captain.

"…good start," Coach Franks continued. "Let's take this positive energy and show the Railers exactly who the Rebels are."

"Yes, Coach," we all called back.

It was vitally important to keep the energy going, not to slip into self-doubt or worry about anything outside hockey, but there was that niggling thought in my head that Webber was officiating tonight. We had already agreed to meet up for coffee, but there was the thorny issue of getting a playoff game out of the way first. I didn't know whether he'd be working on any other Boston matchup in the run to the Stanley Cup, but I both hoped, and worried, about that being a fact.

Hoped, because I wanted to see him again. Worried, because I still felt the shadow of the axe over our necks whenever I glanced over and saw him looking at me. Or when our eyes met on a play, or that moment we almost collided as I was chasing a pass to the net. No one had explicitly told me they noticed my preoccupation with knowing where Webber was, probably because I tried my hardest not to make it obvious. But then, all I could think was how could they not notice when all I could think about was him? I wanted to talk to him and touch him, and it wasn't even only for sex—however mind-blowing that had been.

I was looking forward to coffee, another movie, or maybe just talking and finding out all those things about each other that new lovers need to know. How did he take his coffee? Should I have creamer in my refrigerator just in case? Or sugar? I had little sugar in my place or much in the way of processed foods. I was all about eating at the arena or cooking variations of chicken dishes when I was at home. In fact, there was a hell of a lot of chicken in my freezer.

Which side of the bed did he sleep on? Was he exclusively a bottom, or was he versatile? I mostly topped, but for the right person—the one that made me burn as much as Webber did—I'd bend over in a flash. I craved him fucking me into tomorrow. There was an urgent spark in me that called to him, made me hot with a desperate need to touch and to find out if he had an answering fire. The two times we'd been together had been colored by urgency and desire, but what would it be like if we slowed it down? If I spent hours kissing and tracing his body, and—

"Okay. Words done. Let's see some action! Xander?"

Fuck. I'd lost focus on what Coach Franks was telling us, and that was dangerous. I glanced around at the rest of the team, but no one was looking at me with expectation as if they wanted me to offer additional information or answer a question.

"Lyamin is slow to the left," Xander observed and didn't have to say anything else, nodding to Sergei, our goalie, who took the tablet from him and watched the play.

"Agreed," Sergei said with a frown. I know for a fact that Lyamin and Sergei were buddies, part of an insane goalie WhatsApp group that no one had known existed until the goalie for Vancouver accidentally shared a screenshot. The goalies had been debating hotly about the best Elvis movie, and it was both hilarious and ever so slightly scary.

"Don't make it obvious, but go for top left," Xander directed this at Austin, who nodded in all seriousness.

"Top left," Austin agreed. Say something like that to any other player, and it would be more a wish than a certainty, but Austin had a growing experience of being deadly accurate when he got the chance. Were the Railers looking at game film and having the same conversation about perceived weaknesses in us? Slightly hysterical, I considered for a moment if they were discussing the fact that the Rebels' third-line center kept staring at the referee.

A meaty hand slapped down on my leg, and I glanced up at Marquis as he used me to lever himself to stand.

"The fuck? Asshole!" I cursed and batted his hand off, only he gripped my thigh once before releasing me.

"Head in the game, dude, head in the game." He didn't shout the words, and they were lost in the general noise of a hockey team heading back to the ice. No one else said anything, but if *he'd* noticed I'd drifted off, then it wouldn't be long before somebody else did. I cracked my neck and shoved him.

"Head's always in the fucking game!" I said and grinned at him as if everything was totally okay and I wasn't freaking out that my staring had been noticed. I blew him a kiss. He caught it and pretended to pocket it, and then shoved me back.

"Fuck you, Lomac," he snorted.

We got into a kind of mini wrestling match as we made our way to the lineup in the corridor, tapping each other's calves and working ourselves up to an adrenaline overload. "Fuck you back!"

With only a few minutes left in this first game of the potential seven, I was having way more fun than I was supposed to. I couldn't remember the last time I'd enjoyed playing the game as much as this or felt the joy of skating in every cell of me. I was so privileged, so damn lucky to be out here living the dream, and as we all shuffled up the bench with the second line going out on the ice, I couldn't help grinning.

"The fuck is wrong with you?" Marquis commented, lifting his visor, wiping his eyes, and then squirting an energy drink into his mouth. He'd gotten an assist on the second goal tonight, but even he wasn't grinning as manically as me. "We've not won yet."

I could feel it in every cell of me. When Austin went top left on Lyamin and the lamp lit behind the net, there was an inevitability about the whole thing. We were one goal up with only ninety seconds left on the clock. All we had to do was protect the puck at our end, and even though the Railers pushed as hard as they could, when the buzzer sounded, the arena erupted into roars of satisfaction and happiness.

It was the first team to win four games, and game one belonged to the Rebels.

We all crowded around Sergei, knocking helmets with our goalie, who was less pissed now that we'd won, and then we did a quick lap of the ice in thanks to the crowd. I deliberately made a show of not staring at Webber as he and Xander shook hands.

"Game one, baby!" Marquis gripped me in a bear hug, and we danced our way back to the locker room.

Game one! Fuck yes.

I HADN'T BEEN TO THIS COFFEE SHOP BEFORE. THE TEAM went to Bean Town Brews, which wasn't far from the arena. There was even a room that, although not labeled with the Rebels' name, was a quiet space for us all to sit. This shop, however, was slap bang in the middle of tourist central, part of a chain that was less coffee shop, and more bistro with brunch at the top of the menu. I'd left the T and walked the remaining few minutes to the harbor in the warmth of a beautiful Boston morning. As I reached the place, I realized just how much of a tourist destination it was, and for a second, I was confused. Wasn't this dangerous?

Packed to the rafters, it was ten dollars for coffee, and thirty if you wanted to add something to eat. People, literally, lined up out the door simply because of the proximity to the harbor. I realized, then, that this choice of place was a good one on Webber's part. If we'd gone to a back-end-of-nowhere place that only locals knew, chances are I'd be recognized, and maybe him too. This way, I was just another guy in a Red Sox T-shirt with a matching cap. I couldn't see Webber at any of the cramped tables inside or outside, but given the line, I joined it with the rest of the tourists, listening to at least five different languages emanating from the bustling groups and families around me. I could always move aside when I got to the front if Webber hadn't arrived.

"Are you legitimately a Red Sox fan?"

Webber took me by surprise, sliding in to stand next to me. He was dressed much like I was, but he was wearing Yankees gear and looking damn proud of himself at the same time.

"Go Red Sox." I faked a wave. "Wait, are you *actually* a Yankees fan?"

"Since I was old enough to know what baseball was," Webber said with a wink.

I tapped my Red Sox hat. "Me too," I lied. Baseball wasn't really my thing because I was hockey all the way.

He raised a single eyebrow, and I knew he was doubting the veracity of my statement. "And there I was thinking you were in disguise."

I shrugged. My cover had been blown. "You're not wrong. But, when in Boston…"

We exchanged smiles, and he shifted a little closer as people tried to move past, our hands touching. Just that soft touch was enough to have my heart leaping and for my mouth to go dry. I had the insane urge to lace my fingers with his, but I settled for the gentle brush of his fingers and tried not to make it obvious that I wanted more. What we had between us so far felt forbidden, as if I was back in the closet that stifled me from being a teenager and straight on into my marriage. I bet no one in this bistro slash café would even flinch at two men holding hands, but if someone took a photo, and we were in the background, and the NHL found out, and…

Yeah, hashtag secret.

"Is it just because we need to keep this on the down low that makes it so intense?" Webber murmured close to my ear.

My stomach sank. Is that what he thought? Was this insane need I had inside me simply because of the allure of the forbidden? It couldn't be. No. It was more than that. It was a connection on some kind of level that I couldn't even analyze.

"No. It just *is* intense," I murmured back. His eyes widened, and he leaned in closer to me, linking our pinkie fingers. Just his touch was enough to have me swaying back. This was it. We were going to kiss in the middle of a tourist hotspot and—

"What can I get you?"

I snapped out of the lean, startled by the barista/server asking us for our order, semi thankful that she'd stopped us from kissing, and also irrationally disappointed. Webber was similarly conflicted with his frown, although he got his words out, which was better than I did.

"Coffee, cream, sugar, and a stack of pancakes with syrup and bacon. I'm assuming it's real maple syrup?" The assistant nodded, then looked at me expectantly. I wasn't able to be as adventurous in the realms of sugar as Webber clearly was, but I had a sweet tooth as much as he did.

"Espresso, and can I get French toast with a side of bacon? We'll take one table at the back, please."

"If you poke this into the upturned flowerpot, the server will find you." She handed us a wooden spoon with the number ten on it, which was quirky, and before I could pull out my card to pay, Webber was there.

"I'll get the next one," I reassured him because I knew there would be a next one, and one after that, and hopefully, many more following, as I selfishly wanted breakfast with Webber every day. I was insane with the craving to wake up next to him. *So, fucked*.

Despite the heaving hordes of tourists, I noticed most of them didn't stay long, checking their long lists of things they wanted to see and do in their possibly limited time in the city. That meant the tables right at the back in the corner were empty, so that's exactly where I headed, with Webber directly behind me. I chose the seat that would have my back to the room, more by luck than with any hint of self-preservation. Webber took the chair opposite, then removed his cap and laid it in his lap before ruffling his dark hair as if that was going to tidy it all up. I just thought his cap hair was so damn cute.

"So, do you come here often?" I joked, and he raised a single eyebrow.

"Usually, I find the most out of the way hole-in-the–wall-type place, typically attached to a bookshop. This is my idea of..." he leaned in a little, and I copied him, "hell."

Someone bumped into my chair. A young kid was trying to clamber up my side, and an apologetic mother grabbed him, looking frazzled. "Sorry. Sorry. Benny, come on, we need to get back on the Duck Tour."

Little Benny wasn't happy about that. "I don't wanna!" he whined, and I exchanged sympathetic glances with the mother, who rolled her eyes in exasperation at her son.

"Do you have kids?" Webber asked cautiously.

"No. We always planned on it one day, but no. You?"

"Never found the right guy to settle down with to want to have a family," he replied, and I wanted to grab him right then and hug him hard. He sounded thoughtful with a helping of maudlin.

Coffee arriving curtailed our chat, and I watched in fascination as Webber added cream and sugar to his, tasting it and wincing, before adding another teaspoon of white crystals.

"It's my one vice," he muttered defensively, but I didn't care if he wanted to add half a pound of sugar to his coffee. I was just happy I was here.

"Cheesecake," I announced.

"What about it?" He stirred his coffee again, and this time, when he sipped, he seemed satisfied with whatever alchemy he'd performed.

"It's the one thing I'll break the diet for. Plain

cheesecake, nothing fancy, and not the baked kind, but the type made with cream cheese. I could eat the whole thing."

Webber sat back in his chair, relaxing. "That's what retirement is for Mr. NHL." I couldn't help wincing at what he was saying because, not only were we out in a cafe with *people*, but also he'd hit the proverbial nail on the head of my current indecision. Another year with the Rebels sounded good, but if they traded me, then I could end up in Shittsville, and I didn't want that at all. So, I changed the subject.

"Within a month of me giving up hockey, I'll have a cheesecake belly." I lifted the hem of my T-shirt and patted my tummy, glancing up at Webber, who had his coffee halfway to his mouth, his eyes wide. He cleared his throat and put the coffee back down.

"Fuck," he muttered and leaned into me. "Do you know how much the thought of you with a cheesecake belly turns me on?"

I swallowed. "Cheesecake belly is a turn-on?"

He paused for a moment, capturing his lower lip between his teeth, then releasing it. Deliberately, *sensually*, he ran the tip of his tongue over that same spot. I was so hard that I wriggled just to relieve some of the pressure. He must have known what he was doing to me. "Anything connected to you is a turn-on," he finally half-whispered and nudged my foot with his own. "If we weren't trying to be sensible…"

"Are we? Are we being sensible, I mean? I'm playing in a professional final, and you are in a position where I could take advantage. That's not sensible at all. That's the definition of insanity."

He shrugged, but I knew he wasn't dismissing the point, more like he was agreeing with it, but was choosing to ignore it for breakfast today. As if this one day was vitally important.

The server interrupted us when he arrived with breakfast. I didn't start mine until I'd watched Webber pour the little jug of syrup all over the three fluffy pancakes. If I'd thought he was sexy with all the noises he made when I was fucking him in a bathroom, then the way he sighed and made appreciative sounds about maple syrup pancakes was even sexier. I couldn't just sit here and stare at him as much as I wanted to, cataloging the way his hair fell around his face or the way his lips were shiny with syrup or how his gaze would flick up to mine, humor in the chocolate depths. He knew exactly what effect he was having on me, and I forced myself to ignore him long enough to get a mouthful of French toast.

"You're missing out not having the syrup," he said, then speared a small part of my French toast, dipping it in the syrup before offering it to me. I didn't even think about who might be watching, or what they might be thinking. I'm not entirely sure friends feed other friends breakfast from their own forks. Still, it didn't stop me from leaning in and eating that tiny morsel, making exaggerated appreciative noises that had Webber's eyes widening.

"We really need to leave," he said, his voice sounding husky.

"As soon as we finish this," I teased.

I've never seen two grown men clear their plates and drink their coffees as fast as Webber and I did.

And then we were out of there faster than a Rowe on a breakaway.

Chapter Nine

Webber

ONE OF THE MOST BEAUTIFUL THINGS, IN MY OPINION, WAS to see the rose-colored hues of dawn warming a bare, strong, male back.

I'd come awake a few minutes ago, groggy, tender in delicate places, and slightly confused about where I was. The hotel rooms all started to look the same after so many years, but the sturdy, warm body next to me had been new. That had given my sluggish brain a bit of a jolt until the memories of last night flooded over me. Then, I smiled softly and rolled to my side to witness dawn breaking early over Logan's muscular back. Moving gently to not wake him, I laid there contentedly, staring at the ridges, dips, and valleys of his shoulders and spine. The blankets were low on his hips, exposing a cleft above his chunky ass that had begged to be touched. And so, I had, delicately, with just the tip of my index finger. I followed the valley between his buttocks down, then back up, enjoying the soft blond hairs gliding over the back of my knuckles.

"You looking to start something?" Logan's craggy voice broke the morning silence. He moved to his side as he tossed the covers back. With a proud jerk of his chin down at his hard prick, he offered the stiff shank of meat to me.

I was not a foolish man. If someone presented me with such a gift, I would not turn it down. Placing a hand on his pectoral, I pushed his shoulders back into the mattress before slinging myself over him, my lips going to his jaw to drop tiny kisses along his scruffy chin and down to his throat.

"I love the way you use your mouth." He sighed, the muscles under my hands relaxing as I tasted my way down his chest, stopping to mouth and suck on each dark pink nipple. His big body squirmed and writhed.

"You ain't seen nothing yet," I replied breathlessly. My need to have him take my mouth as he had my ass last night overwhelmed me.

He cupped my jaw, his fingertips warm and rough, and tipped my head back so he could look into my eyes. Hell, he might have been gazing into my soul.

"You're something pretty special," he whispered. I had to blink to clear away the rush of emotions that threatened to choke me. I pushed them down hard and fast, telling myself that if anything was going to choke me, it would be his dick. There was no room for feelings in this…whatever it was we were doing. Career suicide was probably the best name for us hooking up all the time. Knowing it was pushing our luck to get together so frequently, I could *not* stop. I needed him terribly, and not just for this. I stroked him firmly, pulling a low growl of pleasure from his big body. No, it was not just sex anymore. It hadn't been since that late-night movie. Something had shifted that night, but I could not vocalize it just yet. That thing that had sprung to life when he showed himself to be more than just a hot fuck was winning me over. Soft laugh by soft laugh, risqué smile by risqué smile.

Instead of replying to his tenderness, I spent all my energy on pleasuring him. Taking him into my mouth so well that he was lost in no time. Once he spilled down my throat, he moved fast like a jungle cat, the speed at odds with his size. With a grunt, he had me on my back as he covered my mouth with his. The kiss was hungry, yet gentle, his tongue roaming my mouth, gathering the lingering taste of himself as his weight settled on me. I carded my fingers into his hair, tugging on it tenderly, which made him moan into my mouth. Then, his mouth left mine. He kissed a smoldering path down to my cock. With a glance up at me that fried all my mental circuitry, he took me apart. He laved attention to every inch of me, his mouth and fingers taking me skyward with haste. It was frightening how fast he had me on the edge. We'd just fucked last night. We'd both found pretty spectacular releases, falling to the bed sweat soaked and winded before curling into each other for what was supposed to be a short rest before he snuck out like a thief in the night.

Recalling last night and how he had held me tight as he came was all it took. I tumbled over the edge, gasping his name as he groaned in pure pleasure. Shudders racked me. My mind flew off to that soft cloudy place it goes after such exquisite bliss. I floated down, my eyes flickering open as he moved back over me, his hairy thighs rubbing mine, his whiskery chin scraping over my tender lips. I nibbled softly. He chortled, then swept in for a deep kiss that left me struggling for breath as I scrabbled to cling to the fraying rope of reality.

He pulled back, holding his weight off my chest with strong arms locked at the elbow. His hair was a knotted mess, his lips puffy, his eyes glazed with lingering passion and something much stronger than lust.

"I should go," he whispered. I nodded. Yes, he should. But I clung to him, pulling at his thick neck until his mouth joined mine. I kept him in my bed for another hour, whispering and kissing, our hands roaming over each other, the light outside growing by the minute. Finally, when we could deny it no longer, he dropped a kiss on my nose and left the bed. I lay under the covers that smelled of his cologne and musky sex, watching him dress, wishing it could be different.

Smiling and waving down at him through the window ten minutes later as he dashed across a busy street, with Boston commuters heading to work, I pulled my robe tighter around me. I stood there for the longest time trying to sort out what the hell I was going to do now. Everything had changed with the realization that I wished what we had could be something other than what it was supposed to be, whatever the hell that even was anymore. All the lines were blurred, and I had no clue how to clarify them. Fans always said refs needed glasses. That was never truer than right now. Did they make spectacles that could help a confused man see more clearly?

A WEEK LATER, I WAS IN WASHINGTON D.C. TAKING A short break between periods of game seven of the Washington/Carolina first-round playoff. I'd landing at Dulles at three in the morning, after jetting away from a triple overtime game in Toronto that Toronto had won. Eventually. Fuck, I was tired. But here I was, in the officials' room after a manic couple of periods of play.

"I swear, if this game goes into overtime, I may lie down at center ice and cry," I told Drew Willoughby, one of the linesmen for tonight's game.

"Yeah, that was one for the books," he replied, dropping down on a bench to knock back an energy drink.

We had a short talk about old goalies, kids playing hockey, and what we were doing with ourselves over the summer. General chitchat, nothing earth-shattering. I glanced up at the clock after demolishing a granola bar and washing it down with a bottle of water.

"Time to get back on the ice," I said as I pushed onto my skates. Michel, the other ref, patted me on the back, his hand slapping on the double fours I wore.

"Sharp eyes, forty-four," he said in a thick French accent. Then, he did the same and said the same to each man in black and white. It was his ritual before each period. We all had our little quirks. Some refs prayed and some simply chilled. I wasn't a religious man, so instead of asking for divine intervention, I rubbed my whistle for luck just to please Michel.

We were on the ice before the players, making a few rounds to check ice conditions, peek in on the other officials, and run through the checklist of things that were our responsibility. The fans were incredibly loud. They wanted their team to win badly. Of course, that could be said of all the fans. The Carolina backers were just as rowdy and energetic. But this barn was humming with energy. Washington had not moved past the first round for several years. Everyone in the arena was starved for a win. We'd see how things went. Right now, everything stood at zero/zero, but that could change on the bounce of a rubber disc. I really hoped someone scored. I was dead on my skates.

The faceoff at center ice was mine. I skated in and gave the two centers the look. They gave me looks right back. Things had been chippy tonight. Nothing terrible, but tempers were short, and the players were tired. Hell, we were all tired. The NHL season was motherfucking long, and by this time, everyone out here was depleted and probably nursing injuries.

"Dragomirov, you look like you're ready to gnaw the leg off a grizzly," I commented to the Washington captain as we moved in for the puck drop.

"Killian's mother's chili just kicked in," Dragomirov tossed out, his grin wide for his opponent. Killian didn't bite.

"Okay, let's keep people's mothers and sisters out of the game," I replied and threw the puck to the ice. Both men pounced on it. I skated in reverse with haste. Carolina won the face-off, and the puck moved down to Michel's end without a single player touching it. Michel whistled and motioned for the icing call. And that was pretty much how the first five minutes of the third period went. Lots of stoppages, starts and stops, and players getting pissy about how long it was taking. I mean, how is that our fault? If they'd stop icing the damn puck things would be flowing better.

Play resumed as it does, and within a minute the momentum swing that Washington had gotten from that goal being denied sparked them big time. They scored what would be the game-winning goal two minutes after the ruckus and clinched their spot to move onto the next round to face the Rebels. With that final matchup in place, we'd probably be hearing from the head of officiating with a new roster of which ref and linesmen went where. It was a split for me as to what I was feeling. On one hand, my heart would love to be back in Boston so I could spend a little time with Logan. On the other hand, I should keep away from Boston and Logan, but I doubted that was going to happen. I was in too deep.

As I lounged in yet another dull hotel room with a cup of decaf iced coffee I'd picked up in the hotel bar, all manner of romantic fluff ran through my sleepy mind. Walking through Boston Common with Logan's hand in mine, the warm spring winds blowing over us. Taking a swan paddle boat ride around the pond at the Public Garden as the sun beat down on our heads. Maybe take in a baseball game at Fenway Park, get shown on the kiss-cam and actually be able to smooch the man in public.

"Yeah, that is the stuff of dreams," I said with a sigh. None of that was likely to take place anytime soon. Logan and I were stuck in this limbo place where we were constantly ignoring the enormous elephant that was not only in the room, but it was also sitting on our shoulders. And that bastard was getting heavy.

I blew out a breath filled with loneliness. Fuck but I was tired of this solitary life. I wanted someone to talk to about it all, but there was no one—not even Logan—because we were pretending that everything was fine when it clearly wasn't. I checked the time, grimaced, and put the call through to Trevor, anyway. He picked up on the second ring.

"Hey," my twin said in greeting. "I knew you were going to call."

"You did not," I replied with a small chuckle. Trevor always lifted my spirits.

"No, I didn't. Why do we not have that twin mental connection?"

"Because we're not identical?"

"That is some bogus shit. Give me a minute to take this downstairs. The boys are sleeping over in our room, and they just went down."

I heard him whispering to his husband, Carl, and then the sounds of him leaving the bed.

"Okay, that's better. Now I can talk." He pit-patted to his kitchen. In my mind's eye, I could see it all…him stepping around toys, and Edgar sprawled on the linoleum, his doggy snores filling the small-but-homey kitchen. I loved their place. I'd wished it were mine for years, but now that Logan and I were doing whatever it was we were doing, I wished for that domesticity even more. The oil painting hanging above the desk in my room caught my attention. "So, you're calling late," he said. "Everything okay?"

"Yeah, everything is fine. Just wanted to touch base. How are the boys?" I settled in with my back against the headboard, feet crossed at the ankles, and listened to my brother prattle on for ten minutes about their two sons and all the mischief an eight-year-old and a five-year-old could get into. It was a *lot* of mischief. Trevor sounded incredibly happy, though.

"...ended up with a jar of peanut butter smeared all over Edgar. The dog was gracious about it and was cleaning himself when Carl walked in. Needless to say, that resulted in a trip to the groomers for Edgar and a long talk with the boys about how we do not slather things with peanut butter, even if you did think the dog would make a good lure for the birds. Thankfully, we found them before they sprinkled birdseed all over the dog. So, lesson learned. When you make a peanut butter log for the birds, do not joke about how your Dachshund is the same shape as a log."

"I don't think I'll be having a dog or kids anytime soon," I replied with a dark air of melancholy. I heard my brother inhale. "Wow, that was depressing. Ignore me, I'm just caught up in the end-of-the-season blues. I am so ready to get out of hotel rooms and spend some time at home, or up with you. This life is...well, you know. Whatever. Pretend I never spoke. Tell me about Carl. How's the new job?"

"Webber, what's wrong?" The concern in his voice was clear.

How the hell could I tell him the truth? That I had finally found a man who had captured my heart, but I wasn't allowed to be with him. What kind of fuckery was that?

"Nothing, honestly. It's been a long season, and I'm not as young as I used to be," I lied and prayed he would buy it.

"Uh-huh." Shit, he didn't buy it. I kind of figured he wouldn't. "Well, you are pretty damn old."

That made me snort with amusement. "I'm ten minutes older than you."

"You're still older, you codger." We both tossed a few soft barbs back and forth, and then, the line went quiet. "Web, all kidding aside. If there is ever anything that you need to talk to me about, anything at all, you know you can, right? I am your twin, after all. My womb was your womb. My casa and all that."

"Thanks, that means a lot, even if it was really poorly said."

"Hey, it's midnight and I've been chasing kids all day. Give me a break. I'll be more poetic in the morning. You okay?"

"I'm good. Much better after talking to you. Go to bed."

"Okay, but you reach out if you need me."

"I will. Now get some sleep. Give Carl and the boys hugs from me. I'll see you soon."

"Love you, big brother."

"Ten minutes."

That made him snicker softly before ending the call. The smile on my face melted away within moments. I still needed a little more, so I messaged Logan. I needed that hit before I went to bed.

You around? Need to talk. Miss you. ~ W

Chapter Ten

Logan

SETTLING BACK ON THE BED, I CONNECTED TO WEBBER, who'd just finished with the final game in the Washington/Carolina series. I was nervous and excited, and so damn happy to whoever had invented tablets we could use to talk to each other.

I was even more excited to receive the message asking to talk.

"I don't know whether to be happy you made it out of the arena alive or pissed that we're facing Washington next," I teased as soon as I saw his face. However, the minute the words left my mouth, I regretted saying them. "I'm not *actually* pissed," I hurried to clarify. "And it's not that you doing your job or me doing mine is in any way connected to what the two of us are doing together." I tripped over my words. Webber rolled his eyes as he scooted back on the bed. The screen was moving around as he got himself comfortable and settled into the pillows.

When he finally rested it on his knees, and after a few final adjustments, he seemed happy. This wasn't exactly the same as meeting face-to-face, but whatever we had going on between us had gotten to the stage where we couldn't go a few days without talking to each other.

If I didn't see him or at least talk to him, then my day didn't seem quite right. I know the run for the Cup was the big thing and took up most of my thought process, but knowing that he was there, just at the other end of the line, was a comfort.

A hot, sexy, need-you-now kind of comfort.

"Well, look at it this way," Webber began as if he'd given this a significant amount of thought. "I don't know whether to be happy you beat the Railers or pissed that I've now got to deal with you playing Washington."

He laughed. I joined in alongside him, and just like that, we were back on even ground. We'd not only acknowledged the elephant in the room, but we'd shoved it back into a big box. Apart from him shoving it aside to add one thing.

"Proud of you, Logan. Saw some of the plays on the app. You did good."

My heart expanded with pride. "Thank you. It was… yeah…a good game."

"Anyway, back to real life," he murmured.

Yeah. Real life where there is no mention of hockey. Hockey had always been my entire life, and in any past relationship I'd had, hockey had been at the center of everything. If some random stranger talked about the weather, you could bet I'd start explaining how heat and barometric pressure affected arena ice because I always felt that the game was all I had the authority to talk about. But, given that Webber and I had been trying our hardest to avoid the aforementioned elephant, I realized I had way more interests than I thought.

Who knew that I had so much to say on climate control or how much I knew about the Kingdom of Norstoe through Marquis and Kaleb, his prince?

And Webber knew a lot about everything. I loved to listen to him, which qualified as another interest, right? He didn't quite have the encyclopedic knowledge of Queen's backlist as I did, but we both agreed that "Bohemian Rhapsody" was a thing of genius. Also, that Rami Malek played an excellent Freddie Mercury. We both loved bagels, his with cream cheese and salmon, mine with peanut butter, and only on a cheat day. I wasn't as fixated on my diet as some of the new kids coming in, but I needed to look after myself. Something that Webber appeared to appreciate me doing when he'd spent our last hurried hookup licking his way around my abs as if I was an ice cream cone. Apparently, I had superb and sexy delineation of muscle, or at least that is what he was praising as he paused and glanced up at me, his eyes dark with lust.

Don't think about long words or sex right now.

"Where are you?" I changed the subject, but I didn't need to know he was *in* a hotel, more about which hotel. Officiating at the Washington/Carolina matchup in Washington itself was far enough away from New Jersey for him to be staying overnight, but I'd never asked him what type of accommodations he and the other officials stayed in.

"Hampton Inn, a pool for the morning, and I'd give the bed a nine."

"You swim at hotels?" I sounded surprised, and he frowned.

"You don't?"

"No, I do, if we have time, but only really early when no one else is there. I didn't mean that I don't swim, just that I was interested in knowing what you did at hotels," I explained, tripping over my words and making it sound as if I was asking him exactly what he *did* in hotels. Fuck, this talking over tablets wasn't starting out the best. I was hard from recalling him licking my abs—hell, I was hard even thinking about this call, let alone actually seeing and talking to him. But asking him what he got up to when he was in a hotel was wandering toward dangerous territory. Not only could I imagine him getting off, but did he have other men in his room? Did he hookup with other officials? Was that ethical, either? Did he have a sailor in every port?

Why am I losing it?

"Stop overthinking," Webber murmured. "I get to the hotel, typically exhausted and running on fumes. I sleep alone, I eat alone, I swim early, and I leave to go to the next game or home or to the next hotel."

"I wasn't overthinking, I was…shit, yeah, I guess I was overthinking."

He hesitated for a moment, reaching back to plump up a pillow, and settled back with a thoughtful expression. "We should talk about this."

Jeez. Do we have to? "About my overthinking?"

"No, it's more about…look, when I'm with someone,

I'm *with* them. I don't do sharing; I don't get with other guys; I'm an old-fashioned exclusive guy, and if that isn't what—"

"Me too," I interrupted. "I'm committed to this."

"You're *committed* to me?" He smiled.

I could feel my cheeks redden and hoped it wasn't obvious in the pixels he could see of me. "If committed means I don't want anyone else; I don't need anyone else; and I will kill anyone who even looks at you, then yes, I'm committed." I may sound fierce, but Webber was someone I really wanted in my life.

He blinked at me for a few moments, and I swear the embarrassment radiating from me was enough to heat my entire house. He had to see how red I was.

Finally, he cleared his throat. "You're different."

"Different how?"

"You mean something to me, like what we have could be special and real."

I swallowed. It was as if he was reading my thoughts. "Me too. You're...we're...it's good." *Great finish, not.* "I want to see you, talk to you, sleep with you, and I want it to not be a secret, even though I know it has to be."

He sighed. "After the finals, can we be honest with everyone? We could—"

"Yeah," I agreed to his unspoken words that made him so introspective. "I want to tell my friends, the team, I want to hold your hand and it not be a secret and see if what we have is as real as I want it to be."

He didn't even pause. "Same."

We smiled stupidly at each other, and I wished I could reach through and hold him close. Instead, I settled for changing the subject before I got the first flight from here to Carolina just so I could kiss him.

"Tell me about the room," I said.

"Big bed, drapes, desk, drawers, bathroom."

"The usual then?"

"Yeah. We're on a secure floor."

Hockey players or referees weren't rock stars, but there was still the thorny issue of security for fans who wanted to follow us back from the game. If I recall right, the last time we were in Washington, the hotel we used had two entire floors that were blocked off to anyone outside the teams. If he was in the same hotel as the Rebels one day, I would love to think I could sneak into his room, but stupid was *not* my middle name.

"Good to know you're safe from any marauding Carolina fans," I joked, even as I realized I'd brought the entire conversation back to hockey.

"They weren't overly happy to lose, no." He paused, then changed the subject. "Are you at home?"

"Chilling." *On a high from beating the Railers.* I had so much I wanted to share with him about the respectful way the Railers acknowledged defeat and the way we all shook hands, and how Austin and Ten hugged right there in the middle of the ice. Or that Sergei and Stan had stood in the hallway post-game and talked all kinds of serious in a flurry of Russian for at least fifteen minutes. They might not have even been talking about hockey, but if they had been, then that was now on the list of things to avoid talking about. I couldn't help but sigh. Why was it that the first time I met someone whom I'd wanted to know everything about, I was in a situation as messed up as this?

"I miss you," Webber interrupted my spiraling worries. "I don't know what's happening here, but I miss you so bad, and I don't just mean the sex either."

Webber was deadly serious, and I owed him honesty. "I miss you too. And not just the sex, which is fucking amazing. I miss…everything. Coffee, cake, kissing, and all the C-words."

He snorted a laugh. "You realize kissing starts with a K?"

"Semantics." I smiled at him, and he smiled back. And it was *everything*. "The C word I really wanted to use was cock. But I thought that was tacky."

"Cock is an excellent word." He shuffled on the bed and pulled his tablet closer. I knew he didn't share a room when he was on the road, but unlike me in my cozy apartment, he would have people next door. "I was hoping we could talk about what ours could do right now. Together."

"I love what you can do with yours." I used my best pornographic voice. It was possibly the worst segue to phone sex that I'd ever heard, and it made me snigger. "Okay, so I'm not very good at this phone sex thing."

"I didn't realize we were having phone sex," Webber teased, but we both knew where this was going to end—hopefully with both of us getting off.

"It's been at least four days."

"Four days, three hours," Webber checked his watch, "fifteen minutes, give or take a minute."

"You're making that up."

"Referees never make up things," he said, and it was just the most perfect teasing kind of banter. And yes, I was turned on, and yes, I was so getting off on this. But mostly he made me laugh, he centered me, and I really wished he was here with me right now.

"What are you wearing?" He waggled his eyebrows again, and my cock went from hard to iron in a second.

"My Rebels T, and that's it."

"Show me…"

ROUND TWO, GAME ONE, AND WE WERE IN THE RACE TO the Stanley Cup finals and facing Washington fresh from their success against Carolina. With them having the home advantage, we were in their barn and there was scarlet everywhere. Everyone from pundit to Twitter warrior to people on the street said this was Washington's game to lose, and that it was likely that Washington would be going through to the next round. Mostly, they said the Rebels weren't physical enough, and Washington would stamp all over us. Still, never discount an underdog because, by the end of the second period, we had three goals and Washington had nothing. A big fat zero. Sergei was on fire in the net. Our defense was a brick wall in front of him, and the team had fused into one for a singularly perfect game.

Of course, we messed up some, both sides did, but somehow our mess-ups weren't as bad as theirs. Where we had a turnover, they had two. When we stopped a goal, they let one in. It was a dispirited Washington team that left the ice at the final buzzer, with our four to nothing win in the bag. I desperately wanted to call Webber, but I couldn't; although, I had a message from him waiting for me. He was in my phone under the name Z, short for zebra, which was as close as I could get without giving away who he was or what he did, but I was still nervous someone would figure it out.

"…love you, Isaac, kiss Sophie for me," Joachim said as he made kissy faces. I watched enviously as he and other guys on the team called their partners to share their success. What must it be like not to be having an affair with someone who might hold the future of the team in his hands?

Dramatic hockey player is dramatic.

I sent a quick thank you to his message of congratulations, and for now, that was all I could manage. I called Chloe, but she was on shift, and that meant she couldn't talk. She was happy for me, enthusiastic, and blew me a kiss, but then I was done.

"Jesus, they don't hold back, do they?" Marquis muttered next to me and thrust his phone under my nose. "Apparently, we played dirty according to user WashOneTom7—what kind of handle is that—he's got a bug up his ass about the refs brown-nosing players, hashtag biased."

"What?" I wasn't looking at the phone. I was staring at Marquis, who shrugged. Someone was implying the referees were biased. That happened so much, but right now, that was too close to home. Had this random stranger mentioned names? Was it me? Was it Webber? *Shit, I am losing it.* Webber wasn't even here at this game, so it couldn't be anything to do with him. Or him and me. My heart was racing, my chest tight, and Marquis waved a hand in front of my face.

"You okay, dude?"

"Yeah, sure, of course."

"Keyboard warriors saying that Kaleb bought the game for me with all his billions, given that he owns a castle, blah, blah, blah. If only they knew how not rich the principality is. Not to mention, who the fuck thinks you can mess with the officials in a game?"

I wasn't following the bit about the prince only because I was focusing so much on the officials, but I had to be super careful not to expose my worries.

"Yeah, prince. Poor. Got it."

Marquis stared at me for a moment in shock, then shoved me. "Fuck off, asshole." He was pissed at my dismissal, and he had every right to be. I failed at what to say to make things better, but by the time I got my head round it, he'd stalked off to the showers.

Great. Way to go, Logan. I needed to keep my head in the game, not start worrying about what people *might* say out there that could connect me and Webber. The chances of that happening, with all the care we'd been taking, were close to zero.

I followed Marquis into the showers, intent on apologizing, but the closest shower to him was three down. I couldn't barge in and have a naked face-to-face, so I held back until he'd finished and emerged with a towel wrapped around his waist. He narrowed his eyes at me when I extended a fist to bump.

"I was distracted and wasn't listening. Kaleb is cool."

He actually bumped me back, then hip-checked me

into the tiles. "Get a shower. You stink," he muttered and winked at me.

I really had to keep a lid on my thoughts and emotions right now.

Hockey was the thing.

Hockey was what I was paid to do, and I was determined to do it well.

Chapter Eleven

Webber

FATE, BEING THE TWISTED BASTARD THAT HE WAS, HAD ME calling the sixth Washington/Rebels game. I'd flown into Logan airport after a mad dash from down south somewhere. Where the hell had I been? Florida? Yes, the game had rolled into overtime. Playoff overtime was different from regular season overtime. In the post season, we got a twenty-minute break after the final buzzer of the third. Then we would play for another twenty minutes. Not like in the regular season where we took a fast TV break and then dove into three-on-three hockey for five minutes, followed by a shootout if no goal was scored in the five-minute OT period.

The twenty-minute break was good. We all got our legs back under us as best we could, by rehydrating, using the bathroom, and getting a quick bite if we were lagging in energy. Protein bars were generally washed down with electrolyte drinks. But, on the opposing side, the game dragged on much longer. And make no mistake, every man on that ice was exhausted by this point. Eighty games took a toll. Still, we had a job to do, fatigue be damned.

When I'd landed at the airport, I grabbed my bags and took a taxi to my hotel. It was a new one—well, new for me—but much older than the ones I usually bedded down in. The historic redbrick building was charming and warm, with dark wood paneling, a rowdy bar filled with Boston fans cheering on the Red Sox, and ten rooms that were filled with colonial furnishings. Perhaps, it had been folly to book here, but for once, I wanted to fall into a soft bed with Logan in a setting that wasn't hotel drab. Being with him was special. Call me a fool, but so be it. There was a back entrance that led right into a cobblestone alley that he could sneak out into during the night.

I took a warm shower, went down to the bar to have a light lunch, returned to my room to nap, and called a ride to take me to the arena for the game. The pallor of loneliness that had been dragging me down of late had lessened. I was in Boston. Logan was here. Tonight, after the game, Logan and I would be engulfed in a downy soft bed, naked, loving the hell out of each other. I was buzzed about seeing him again. As much as I loved my job and hockey, summer break could not come soon enough. Just being able to linger in bed with Logan sounded incredible. Maybe taking a trip home with him at my side. Everything seemed possible if we could just make it through the postseason. Then, we could rest, heal our weary bodies, and plan out what we were doing if anything. Maybe, we'd both decide that our affair was too much work and worry. Perhaps, he would call it quits. Maybe I would. Hell, maybe we both would retire and go live in a cabin in the Ontario wilds. He looked good in his playoff beard. Maybe we could trap and hunt the woodlands. Be real mountain men and all that. Or not. I wasn't sure I wanted to live off bear meat, but I was sure I wanted to have Logan Mackie in my bed every night. God, I could not *wait* until tonight!

"You look chipper," my fellow ref said when I strolled into the refs' room. Michel Laroy—pronounced Me-Shell Lere-Wah—was always quick to remind those who liked to butcher his name—gave me a smile. The two linesmen looked up from their phones and nodded. I gave them all a clap on the shoulder as I sat down to take off my sneakers. "Did you get some nookie?"

"No, no nookie, just a good meal and a long nap," I replied with a wink. "Which is sometimes nearly as good as nookie."

We all laughed, then returned to gearing up. That entailed shin pads, protective girdles, elbow pads, a jockstrap, and a CSA-approved helmet, black, with a visor. Our pants had to be black, our skate laces new and white, and our sweater had to be clean with no visible tears or holes, and our names and numbers on the back. Skates must be polished. We all dressed and chatted, mostly about our families or things outside of hockey for a bit, but then, we talked about the upcoming game and our roles in it. I'd previously worked with all the men here tonight, so it was a pleasant, but professional discussion.

When it was time, we headed out, took care of the jobs we were responsible for, then enjoyed the team warm-ups. We were required to be on the ice whenever the players were. This was not a problem at all for me, as it gave me a chance to watch Logan. We nodded at each other from a distance as he and the Rebels took light shots at their goalie. This barn was packed full, which was nothing new, as the Rebels sold out every night. Boston fans were diehards.

"Hey, ref, you going to make good calls for me tonight?" the Washington captain teased as I lingered by the timekeeper's table with a bottle of water, my eyes darting to Logan far more than they should, but I couldn't seem to stop them.

"I don't think I've ever made a bad one," I joked with the big Russian.

He laughed, and we made small talk for a bit. When he skated off to rejoin his team, I looked up to find Logan staring at me with a smoldering fire that held no small amount of possessiveness. My dick jumped. I chided it strongly. A hard-on while wearing a cup was not at all comfortable. This was the side of the game that most fans didn't see, the back-and-forth between players and officials. Most of the time, during the televised games, all the fans saw were players getting into our faces. And yes, that happened all the time. Passions ran high, especially in the postseason, but most of the time the officials and the players had a respectful relationship. Many of them I could call my friends, even though associating with players outside of the rink was discouraged for obvious reasons. I raised an eyebrow in reply to Mr. Mackie. It was truly amazing how much could be said with no words spoken. God knows that one look had lit a fire in my belly for later tonight...

Puck drop was later than usual as the Rebels were

paying tribute to a fallen member of the Boston Police Department. Just a few minutes, but it was enough to feel the energy in the barn starting to climb. The Rebels were up three to two in the series. Washington was up against the wall, knowing that they had to win this one or they'd be golfing tomorrow. Energy rode the cold air as the anthem was being sung.

I skated out with a puck in hand to meet the boys at center ice.

"Gentlemen, let's play clean hockey. Best of luck to both teams." A Washington player edged up. I gave him a look, and he moved back. That happened twice before I waved him out to bring in another forward. "I know you boys are antsy, but no encroaching until the puck drops. This isn't peewee…we all know the rules."

Xander Holden chirped to the Washington player, then bent down all smiles. I knew the Rebels were feeling their oats. They'd pretty much dominated the series from the highlights that I'd watched. It had been a clean set of games so far, for the most part. Only minor infractions, but I suspected things might get a little rougher tonight with so much on the line. We officials had discussed that during our pre-game chat, and we had our eyes on the guys who we felt might be looking to tip the odds in their favor with a sneaky, dirty hit. Most of the men here were good players, but there were a couple who were known offenders with suspensions on their rap sheets.

When the puck finally hit the ice, I moved out of the gameplay and let things take off. The fans were on their feet already, stomping and shouting, and filling the barn with enough electricity to power the city of Boston throughout the game. With the game now started, I eased back to my end, ready to do my job to the best of my ability.

The first period was scrappy. Washington wanted to flex their muscles a bit early on, and after a few stick-handling calls—keep those sticks on the ice, boys—Washington's coach reined in his players a bit. We went to the locker rooms with two goose eggs on the scoreboard. After a short break and a granola bar, we were back at it. The second period was just as physical. The players were playing clean and finishing their checks but keeping things above board. Dad would be happy with how we'd shown the men who was in charge.

The second period was a repeat of the first, with lots of defense, which meant the shots on goal were low. The coaches had to be happy, but the fans were growing irritated. A holding call at the top of the third against Boston got the fans riled up.

"This isn't the ballroom at the Waldorf Astoria, Miller. You can't have your arms around him," I explained to Marquis Miller as we made our way to the penalty box.

"There was no holding," he argued because of course he did. He had to. I got that.

"It was subtle, but I saw it," I replied. He muttered but went to sit his ass down.

"Good call," Michel said when he skated up to me as the penalty was called by the announcer. The fans all booed. "Good call, clean, nice. He knew he was getting frisky."

I chuckled. "He'd get his face slapped if he'd been feeling up a young lady like that," I parried, which made

Michel laugh softly even as the Rebels and their fans were irate. Play resumed after that holding call, but the aura of the arena had changed.

Everyone was edgy. The coaches were bitching at us. The fans were bitching at us, and the players were bitching at us. We kept the lid on for as long as we could, but you could sense something in the air. It was like right before a thunderstorm forms and the air begins to crackle with ominous intent. I felt it on the back of my sweaty neck as the game finally began to roll along with fewer whistles. Four or so minutes of steady action back and forth between both ends of the ice kept us busy. Washington was just coming off a line change when their star forward juked and jived as he hit the ice, trying to steal the puck from Austin Rowe, but his little show didn't work. Rowe, who was setting all kinds of records in the postseason, broke free with the puck and carried it down the ice with speed. Washington's lone defenseman was caught snoozing and had to reach out from behind to grab Rowe's jersey, which impeded Rowe's chance to take a clean shot on net.

The infraction was easily seen, and the penalty was given. Arms crossed over my head after blowing the whistle, I gave Boston the penalty shot. Rowe looked cool as a cucumber, but his guts had to be tight as he picked up the puck at center ice. With the sleek grace that all Rowe men seemed to possess, Austin threw his shoulder left, and the Washington goalie took the bait, leaning left, then trying to move right as he saw Rowe's body shift. The shot was a blur as it streaked past the goalie's mitt and into the back of the net. The Boston bench erupted. Washington's coach was beyond irate and called me over. I had no clue what he thought he was going to gain from the histrionics. Everyone and their beagle had seen the infraction. It was hard to miss a player being pulled down to the ice. After a warning for the coach to watch his language as he spoke to me, the old D-man cooled off. A little. The fact that they were arguing such a blatant interference call was puzzling, but their season was on the line, so I gave them a pass.

That penalty shot was all Boston needed to ramp themselves up. They played solid defensive hockey for the remainder of the period and went on to win, ensuring they would go to the next round.

And Washington was out of the Stanley Cup race.

Leaving the ice after the buzzer, the Washington fans in attendance pelted me with insults. Nothing new there. Anytime a call is made, whether controversial or straightforward like the one I'd called, stirs the pot. We officials did our best to ignore all the posturing and yelling on social media. I personally read zero sports sites, and I never listened to any podcasts about our sport, unless it was something huge.

I'd just stepped out of the shower at the barn when Michel glanced up from his phone with a look of concern.

"Have you seen the papers?" He passed me his cell. I smiled at the older man calling the internet the papers. The smile left my face as I read over the headline. A trickle of water ran down from my wet hair over my spine, making me shiver. "This here guy, this WashTon7 person, is making some pretty ugly accusations about you and that penalty shot call."

I passed the cell back, refusing to read the rest. If refs

looked at every post made about them, there wouldn't be any refs left.

I took the towel from around my shoulders and scrubbed it over my head. "It was bound to raise some hackles. The call was fair, and I stand by it." I looked down at Michel, who was fully dressed aside from his shoes. He was wearing socks with smiling suns on them. That struck me as funny for some bizarre reason. Michel was a nice man, but not exactly what I would call sunny. "You agree, right? It was overt interference on a player that directly impeded a clear scoring shot on a breakaway. I mean, shit, it was textbook. Why are they harping about it?"

"Yes, yes, of course. It was the correct call. We all agreed. Toronto agreed as well. No worries on that, but this article..." He rubbed his rather big nose, his sight darting from my face to my Crocs. "Well, it is not complimentary. This fool is hinting that you may have thrown the call to give favor to Boston."

"What? That makes no sense. First of all, I have never shown any kind of favoritism to any team. Second, that was blatant holding, there was no room for any other understanding. What the hell is he insinuating?"

"That you showed favor from an official," he whispered, clearly uncomfortable. "Whoever this is says that you and Logan Mackie are close friends."

Shit. Oh shit. Shit. Shit. "We're not what I would call friends. We see each other on the ice."

Michel nodded, but still would not look at me. "Yes, that is of course what I am thinking. But whoever

WashTon7 is…well, he says that you are *intimate* friends. That is the term he used in the article. Intimate."

"What?"

Michel cleared his throat and read from the post. "So perhaps a certain ref who is intimate friends with a Boston player might place a finger on the scale to ensure the team said intimate friend plays on will win."

Holy. Fucking. Hell. "That's fucking horseshit." He muttered something in French that I could roughly translate. While those of us from Ontario mostly spoke English, we knew enough French to converse awkwardly. "Do you believe this post?"

His tired blue eyes finally rose to my face. "I do not. But it doesn't matter what I believe, Webber. What matters is what the league believes. And there's a picture…"

Picture? Fuck. Fuck. Fuck. "What kind of picture?"

Chapter Twelve

Logan

FACING OFF AGAINST YOUR OLD TEAM AND THEN BEATING them was both the best and worst feeling in the world. I'd had friends at Washington, people I used to catch beers with, skaters that I'd taken shots to my body for…friends, and when we lined up to shake hands with our opponents, a few of the shakes turned into bro hugs. Dragomirov pulled me into a close hug as if he wasn't going to let me go.

"Team never should have let you go, Lomac. You've beaten us. Now take it all the way, okay?"

I returned the Washington captain's hug. For all his prickliness on the ice tonight, and his anger at losing, he was still one of the few captains I'd played under whom I actually respected.

"I intend to." I couldn't help but grin. He fake punched me, then fist-bumped me to underscore his respect.

The line moved quickly, and all too soon it was time

for one last lap of the ice, raising our sticks to the fans who were here to celebrate our winning this second round. We didn't know who we were up against next, whether it was Toronto or Calgary, but both of them were opponents that wouldn't be easy to win over. Still, the same could be said for both the Railers and Washington, yet we'd done it. A maximum of fourteen games stood between us and the Stanley Cup, and the excitement in the locker room was loud, full of laughter and jokes and high-fives, everyone quietening only when Coach Franks sauntered in with a wide grin, his assistant coaches close behind.

"Now *that* was hockey," he announced, and everyone paused for a moment until we all glanced at each other and started cheering at the same time. It was far from over—we were exhausted—but we were a step closer, and Boston hadn't won the Cup in a few years. "Austin," Coach shook his head, and I glanced at Austin who couldn't stop smiling, "that last breakaway, the way you pulled that penalty and got the goal? Highlight of the freaking game. Enjoy." I knocked elbows with Austin, exchanged a high-five with Marquis, then the team saluted each other with electrolyte drinks. It was moments like this, surrounded by the team, winning, that made every ache and bruise worth it. Maybe part of it was that I knew Webber was here in the city waiting for me to join him, but I'd never felt so happy in my entire life.

"What did Dragomirov say to you?" Austin asked.

"Just that he wants us to take it all," I summarized. I wasn't about to say the first part where he said he'd wished I'd never left because hockey players didn't do that kind of bragging shit. Still, I put the words away in my pocket and knew I'd examine them in private and feel a hundred kinds of proud of myself.

"Ten said exactly the same thing, and Jamie as well. I think they are proud of me." He glanced over to where Brady was chatting to Joachim, slapping him on the shoulder and congratulating him. I took it from Austin's summary that perhaps Brady hadn't expressed pride in his cousin, and maybe Austin needed that positive affirmation. Only Brady was a defensive coach, and Austin was a forward.

"Brady is too," I said, with all the seniority of someone ten years older than him who'd seen things in this game. The Rowe family might be close, but that didn't mean it had to spill out into the locker room. People could be proud of each other without making it obvious. Hell, people could express a lot of things in life without making it obvious.

I couldn't wait to get out of here and head over to the hotel room. I had so much I wanted to do with Webber. Hug him hard, and kiss him, and tell him how much I've missed him. Then, maybe, we could just sit and hold each other and enjoy the moment of being together. I needed that. I hoped Webber needed it too.

"You're up in the post-game interview, Austin, you too, Lomac," Xander said, and I pulled my thoughts away from Webber as I heard my name and focused on my captain. Why would the press want to see me? I'd played well. I gave it 110 percent, but I'd done nothing flashy. Still, maybe they wanted my perspective because I'd played for Washington and won the Cup as part of last year's team.

"On it," Austin said, pulling a towel around his neck and bouncing to his feet with all the joys of youth. I was slower to stand, my hamstrings tight and burning with lactose, and my right arm ached like fuck. Not that I showed that to anybody, just dutifully followed Xander and Austin across to the media room scrum. I pasted on my meet-the-public smile and took a seat in one of the spare cubbies, three down from Austin and six from Xander. There were already reporters clustered in my spot, and I smiled at them, waiting for the first question. I already had my pre-rehearsed answers for anything they might ask about Washington, about what Dragomirov had whispered to me on the ice, about how I hoped Austin would go all the way and I could lift the Cup with two separate teams.

"Hi, guys." My words were lost in laughter from down at Austin's place, and I didn't quite catch the first question thrown at me. "Say again?"

The interviewer wasn't someone I readily recognized, probably somebody new or maybe someone just in for the Stanley Cup run, but I could read expressions, and his pointed glance suggested he knew something no one else did.

"Are you in an intimate relationship with Webber Kelty?"

"What?"

"The same man who called the contentious penalty that meant Boston won to go through to the next round." He still looked sly, with a faint smile and a flush of enthusiasm that maybe he'd found the story of his life. Everything slowed. How had someone put the two of us together? Who would that be? No one knew. He was fishing. He had to be. Forcing down the panic and keeping my expression neutral, I raised an eyebrow to dismiss the vast majority of the question.

Stick to the hockey. Push down the rest. Don't fucking panic.

"There was nothing contentious about Tillerson yanking at Austin's jersey," I reminded him.

"But you're not denying that you're in a relationship with the same referee who officiated the game tonight."

I gave him my best glare. The one I'd mastered through the limited amount of post-game interviews I'd done. The one that gave the impression I wasn't falling for their shit. "I didn't hear a hockey question in there."

Shit. Shit. Shit. What is going on? Where was Webber? Was he okay? I need to get to Webber. He'll be freaking out.

He rolled his eyes at me, and then, it was the turn of the interviewer next to him to ask me basically the same question, but with the words in a different order. I ignored him and focused on the third interviewer, a young woman with long blond hair, who was smiling at me as if she didn't know what the other two were talking about.

"Ma'am, do you have a question?"

"Are you gay?" she blurted, and I was about done with questions. I wanted to stand up and leave, but the league took these post-game interviews seriously, and I knew I could be fined for walking out. Not that I cared about a fine, but if I walked out now, then wasn't I explicitly admitting to the very thing I was being accused of?

Think. Get out of this.

Someone slipped through the interviewers to stand next to me. The team's media manager, Timo. He was a short, feisty kid who'd been headhunted by the owner from Florida, and who'd turned around the team's social management by being closely involved at the player level. It was Timo who'd encouraged us skaters to have a media presence. It was Timo who helped curate what to share, and it was him standing at my side right now. Just seeing him made what the reporters threw at me feel real. Someone *had* found out about Webber and me. The elation I'd felt from winning the game and the excitement that I was about to see Webber spun into nothing. I was panicking inside, although you wouldn't know it to look at me. I shot Timo a glance, and he stared back at me. There was so much information I took from that simple look. He was in damage control mode— in the same way that he'd dealt with the semi-naked photos of Marquis—and I was terrified about why he was here.

"Hockey questions only, guys, unless you want your media privileges to be reconsidered," he announced, drawing himself to his full height of five-eight, small in a room full of big men, with his arms crossed over his chest. He was smiling, but the smile didn't reach his eyes. The threat was empty. It wasn't as if the team could block the press without it coming over as authoritarian. Despite that, the team could make it uncomfortable for the press to approach a particular player easily. I waited for a hockey question, but hell would have to freeze over before any of the three journalists there would let go of the juicy bone.

"Does the team have a statement to make about the

inappropriate relationship between a referee and a player?" the first one asked.

Timo gripped my arm and tugged me from the scrum. "Interviews are over."

He pulled me out of the locker room entirely and into the player corridor. "No words," he said. "Skip the cooldown, go home, say nothing."

"Wait. Don't you want to know what's—"

"I don't want to know anything." He leveled me with a stare, his jaw tight. "It isn't true because it can't be true. So, fix it," he stated simply. He was telling me that as far as he was concerned—and probably the team—that whatever I'd done hadn't happened. Wasn't happening.

Should stop.

I avoided the team talking about what the media had asked simply because everyone in the room hadn't heard the questions, and Xander and Austin weren't back yet. I did as I was told by showering fast, dressing in my suit, and slinking out of the arena before anyone noticed without signing any autographs. Just sped off into the night, parking some distance from where the hotel room was and walking the rest of the way with my gaze fixed firmly on the ground. The streets in this part of the city were empty at this time of night, all the tourists in the hotspots or safely back in the hotels, so no one stopped me.

Taking the back way into the hotel, I headed straight to the room Webber had booked and knocked twice on the door, still keeping my gaze to the ground, and hoping to hell no one tried to talk to me before I got inside to talk to Webber. My head spun with the horror of being found out, of people thinking they knew what we'd done, and of what Webber would say when he found out.

There was no answer, so I knocked again, and this time, I saw the peephole darken with someone peering out before the door opened slowly to reveal the darkened room beyond. Webber backed away from the door and gestured me inside. Since it was dark, I couldn't even see his face properly, let alone get a handle on his emotions. He didn't pull me into a hug or kiss me, and in my heart, I knew he'd been told about the rumors. I glanced around for the light switch, but after flicking at it uselessly, I realized the room must have one of those systems that needed a key card to connect the electric. A hint of light in the room was coming in from the street, and as my eyes adjusted, it was just enough for me to read Webber's body language.

He was defeated, his posture slumped, and when I reached out to touch him, he stumbled back.

"You shouldn't have come here," he snapped.

Jesus, this was bad. "I had to see you. I just…I had to."

"There's a photo," Webber said. "Have you seen it?" His voice was broken, the world had shattered, and just as I was within touching distance of everything I wanted, my life had become just as fragile.

"I haven't *seen* a thing." I swallowed as I wondered how honest I needed to be. "But after the game, I had questions from the media."

He groaned and slumped to the bed. My eyes had adjusted to the gloom enough that I saw the brilliant white key card on the desk, taking it and slotting it into the reader. Instantly the room filled with light, and I turned off the overhead lights, leaving on just the sidelights to the bed because anything else was just too jarring. I crossed the room to close the drapes and then, locked the door.

"We'll get through this," I murmured. I was determined we would get through this because I'd found him, and he was the one—I was falling in love.

"You should look," he mumbled and handed over his phone.

The screen showed a hockey gossip site dedicated to the Washington team. It was nothing new to me—photos of partners, gossip about trades, photos of the players when they were kids—mostly a happy place and hugely supportive of the team. Unless, of course, the gossip turned nasty, and this inevitably happened whenever a Washington fan was pissed at a loss or felt slighted. Every single team in the NHL had websites like this. Boston's could be just as toxic and even though I tried to ignore them, I'd seen some crap posted about me in the past when I'd been traded into a team or traded out.

I skimmed the words after the click bait headline and found the photo, clicking on it to enlarge it and using my fingers to zoom in. It was an innocent photo, taken back on that first coffee date. Webber and I sitting opposite each other, just chatting. There was nothing in this photo that implied an improper relationship or any kind of relationship for that matter. It was just two friends meeting for coffee.

"Is that all they've got? Jesus, it's not against the law to have coffee with a friend."

"It's you. Can't you see how you're looking at me?"

To be fair, I hadn't checked myself in the photo, too enamored with staring at Webber and thinking just how gorgeous and sexy he looked, all ruffled and smiling at me. I zoomed in on the photo to look at myself, and that was when I saw it. It might have been our first date, but I was looking at him as if I'd fallen in love at first sight. I had such a sappy expression, one that spoke of wanting to kiss Webber, and it wasn't even subtle. Was I reading too much into the photo? Was Webber? Just because I knew how I felt at that moment, and maybe he'd felt something similar, it didn't mean that anyone looking at the photo would think we were an item.

"This shows nothing," I lied. If no one outside of me and Webber knew how we felt about each other, then they wouldn't be able to read that in the expressions in the photo. All they'd see is two friends.

"Fuck that. It might not be obvious to you, but it shows an NHL referee having coffee with someone from the team he'd be refereeing in the lead up to the Stanley Cup. Do you not get it?"

"Webber—"

"Read the article."

That's the last thing I wanted to do but forewarned is forearmed. I sat next to him on the bed and scrolled to the top of the article. The headline hadn't changed. The first paragraph still announced with horror that a player and referee were having an affair. Thing is, they weren't wrong —we were together. We *were* having an affair, but it was more than that.

Paragraph one speculated on my sexuality, linking to articles from players who identified as queer from Boston and other teams. I always knew one day that it would become common knowledge that I was bisexual, but it had never been part of my hockey persona. I was the rental, the one who came in worked hard, kept their head down, and didn't make waves. Who I slept with wasn't so much a secret as a non-thing, and anyway, it was no one's business but my own. I resented the implication that "every hockey player in the league" was coming out as gay, but at least it gave me an insight that the author of this vitriol was coming from a position of prejudice. It should be easy to ignore the rest once I knew that, but I kept reading and each cut from the knife the author wielded was worse than the last.

They referred to rules and regulations and bias and blackmail and made it a million times darker and more impossible than it was. There was nothing in here about trusting that referee and a player could fall in love and not let it affect the game, there was nothing in here that was positive at all.

The summary was the worst. It called for Webber to be relieved of his position and for every call that he'd made in his career to be examined carefully. The implication was that he must have done this before, that he used his sexuality to gain an advantage, and that he was the one using me as a player for some nefarious reason that they didn't explain. I knew he hadn't, but when I glanced up at him, he was on the defensive.

"I've never done this before. I've never compromised myself or my colleagues or the league. You're the only person. You know that."

He was agitated. "Of course, I know that. I'm not stupid." Maybe that wasn't what I was supposed to say because he winced and then closed his eyes. "The call went up to Toronto. It was a blatant holding, and anyone with any hockey sense could see that."

I scrolled lower to read the first few comments. Some were obviously from Boston fans, given their handles, who defended me and Webber and called the whole thing a pack of lies. Washington fans were suggesting Boston had paid off the big guys in Toronto who signed off on any penalties that were in the gray area. But our fans weren't backward at coming forward and saying that the Washington fans were just pissed we knocked them out of the run for the Cup. Some of those comments had become war, and I tried to ignore the hate and nastiness being slung both ways. Then there were comments from Washington fans who agreed with the original poster that Webber had compromised everything. They said that if Webber hadn't been the ref for the game that Washington would have won easily.

Easily? Only the guys on the ice knew how fucking hard the game had been.

And then I saw a comment that made my blood run cold—someone calling for a hitman to take out Webber and show the league how real justice was served and how badly he'd fucked Washington over.

"I'm calling the cops and Boston's social media guy and a lawyer. We'll get a good one, we'll—"

"You need to leave," Webber interrupted and snatched the phone from my hand.

"I'm not going anywhere. Webber, I'm not leaving you. This is all bullshit."

"Is it?" Webber was so intense—furious at himself,

edgy and sparking with anger. "This should have stayed in the bathroom at that bar. Just once and done."

"No. Webber, babe—"

"Don't call me that," he snarled.

"You know how I feel about you. I know that I'm falling in—"

"It's just fucking," Webber said crudely. "I've compromised myself, left myself wide open to criticism for all the things I've done in the past. I deserve that. But us? It was never gonna last, not if I want a career that matters."

"I'll retire," I said quickly, wondering why the solution hadn't been obvious to me before. "Then you won't be in a relationship with an active hockey player. Hell, you could retire. I have more than enough money to—"

"Listen to yourself, Mr. Rich Hockey Player who thinks money is more important than integrity," he snapped.

"I didn't say that. Webber, come on, let's talk about this."

He stood up and yanked at the bolt on the door before opening it wide. "Go."

"Webber…" I stood as close to him as I dared, trying not to let my heartbreak show when he stepped back. "What we have is worth fighting for."

He shook his head. "No. It's not. My career, my reputation, it's everything to me, and I've fucked up. My parents…my dad…shit. When they read this…" he scrubbed his eyes. "You need to leave. I need to think."

We stared at each other, his expression stoic, and I

could feel every single awful emotion pressing heavily on my chest.

"I was falling in love with you," I whispered.

His eyes brightened with emotion, but he shut it down fast. "It could only ever be just fucking. Now leave before I mess anything else up."

"This isn't all on you, this is both of us—"

"You'll ride it easy," he muttered. "Just go." He didn't falter, determined to have me leave. This wasn't over. I'd let him cool down and talk to Timo to get some kind of strategy in place. Maybe a press release from the team, something that would help.

"If you won't talk now, then please call me," I said, but he shook his head. And then, because I didn't have any choice, I headed back to the car. I didn't cry or rail at the asshole who'd posted that shit and split us apart. I carefully drove home, parked the car, and let myself in.

And only then did I lose control, sliding down the wall and sitting with my back to the door. My broken heart escaped in frustrated, angry, heartbroken curses.

Chapter Thirteen

Webber

THAT MIGHT HAVE BEEN THE LONGEST NIGHT OF MY LIFE.

No, no might. It had been. I was still wide awake when the sun rose to begin warming the Boston cityscape. I hadn't slept a wink. All I had done was pace the beautiful room that I'd rented for Logan and me. Each glance at the bed or the cherry wood armoire or the spindly-legged desk made me feel worse and worse. Panic had ridden me hard last night. It was still on my back, driving spurs into my flesh like some demented rider from the depths of Hell.

Sipping on a cup of coffee, who knew how many, I stared out at the sunrise, dreading the dawn, as it would bring the wrath of the league down upon me. And Logan as well.

Every time I recalled his stricken face, my chest constricted. I'd been cruel. And I knew that. I'd been gripped in a spiraling despair of fear that had me lashing out at the one person I should have clung to. The one person I wanted to hold was the one person I had to distance myself from.

Despite how I wanted Logan, how much I craved his touch, and how much I desired to be with him for the rest of my days, that was out of the question. Our careers were at stake. We'd both worked too hard, suffered too many injuries, and spent too many nights alone for the game to simply toss it aside as if it were nothing.

Cradling my mug between my hands, I played a waiting game. My phone sat plugged in on the nightstand beside a box of chocolate-covered cherries I'd picked up at the airport. My plan had been to feed them to Logan, then lick the sweetness from his mouth. Now they were setting there, unopened, a painful reminder of all we had lost. Fucking stupid people. What the hell possessed some fans to be so toxic? What did it matter who I slept with?

Anger welling up inside me did not erase the knowledge that I knew quite well that who I slept with or even associated with off the ice mattered. It mattered because the public would think that an official was biased toward a friend or lover. Logan and I had both known that as soon as we'd understood who the other person was in this hidden affair. Hence, keeping it hidden.

I dropped my brow to the cool window, the AC blowing cold zephyrs into my face. It was just after seven when the first call came through. I turned away from Boston, glowing bright yellow as the late May sun warmed the cobblestones and ye olde brick buildings.

Blowing out a long breath, I padded over to my phone, the empty mug still in my hand, to check the incoming call. Yep, it was Dan Hamilton, the head of officiating.

"Here we go," I said to the still neatly made bed. I tapped the green button to accept that call and put it on speaker. Somehow, my exhausted brain decided that Dan's voice wouldn't be as upsetting if it wasn't right in my ear. As soon as he greeted me, I knew that was not the case at all. His deep voice, thick with Minnesota flavoring, was just as distressing on speaker as it would have been entering my ear. "I think I know what you're calling about."

Dan's exhalation was strong. "I woke up to a firestorm this morning, Webber. Now, given how well I know you, and your father before you, I'm hesitant to even ask if this claim that is setting the sports blog on fire is true, but I feel I have to. Are you having an intimate relationship with Boston Rebels forward Logan Mackie?"

Yep, that was Dan. He did not beat around the bush. He said what he had to say and let the chips fall where they may. This morning the chips were tumbling down on me and my career. I'd spent the night ingesting mass quantities of caffeine, trying to decide how to reply to this question when it arrived. I could lie. That would be the easiest out. Just say no and dare someone to prove that I was anything more than a friend to Logan.

Or.

Or I could be honest and light the fuse that would blow my long, and to this point, immaculate career to bits. What would my father advise me to do?

"Yes, I'm having an intimate relationship with Logan Mackie," I confessed.

Tick, tick, tick.

"I see," Dan icily replied. "I didn't know you were gay."

"Well, I didn't tell anyone, as it has no bearing on my job performance. Do you ask other refs if they're straight?"

"The other refs haven't been caught on camera in a cozy café with a player making small talk and googly eyes at each other."

Boom.

"I would like to say that my being involved with Logan did not in any way influence my calls in any of the games that I officiated."

"Webber, I believe you. I know your lineage. And I am rather sure that the league will believe you as well. That being said, the fans and the press are already howling about you being friends with a player. That alone looks bad. If they find out that you two are dating, then that will be a shitstorm of epic proportions."

"Yes, it will be. I am incredibly sorry, Dan." I didn't know what else to say. Sorry didn't even begin to express the sorrow and shame that I was feeling right now. Dan had been incredibly good to me over the years, and this was how I repaid his kindness. By bringing a tornado of bad press to his front door. The commissioner was probably on a rant of epic magnitude right now. "We didn't mean for this to be an ongoing affair, but…"

"If you lay that old 'the heart wants what the heart wants' bullshit on me right now, I might lose my shit. The heart may want something, but we're grown men who can —or should—be able to control our damn dicks."

"Well, there is a difference between dicks and hearts, Dan," I fired back. Lack of sleep and elevated stress levels make me chippy.

"Not in this instance. If you want to fuck some dude on your time, that is fine. The league and the official's union will march behind you with rainbow flags, but you do *not* stick your dick into a player. Jesus Christ, Webber, you know this. You grew up with one of the most famous and well-respected referees the game has ever known. What the hell is your father going to say when news of this gets out?"

I had no clue what Dad would say. He would be crushed. He'd been so thrilled when I'd chosen to follow in his footsteps...

"I'm so sorry, Dan."

"I know you are, and I'm sorry too. As of today, you're suspended and barred from officiating at any other games. I'm going to have to run this past the commissioner and let you know what his thoughts are, but as of now, I want you to keep a low profile. The press does not know that you and Mackie are lovers, and I want to keep it that way as long as possible. I also would like you to consider exactly what you want out of your future, Webber. Do you want to be an official in the NHL or do you want to be some rental's boyfriend? Seems to me the choice would be an easy one, but you do you."

And just like that, the call ended. I dropped down to the bed, buried my face into the soft down pillows, and rage screamed into the goose down until my throat was sore. Rolling to my back, I stared at the fan overhead, whirring away, moving the cool air down into my red, dry eyes. I wanted to cry but that would get me nowhere.

I moved to my side as my phone buzzed. I ignored it. The world and those upon it could kiss my ass. Knowing that the worst of this mess was just starting to gain momentum, I drew in a shaky breath and forced myself to make one rational decision. The first since that night wearing a Mardi Gras mask. I resigned myself to getting on the first flight to Ontario to speak with my family in person, hopefully, before the ugliness went international. As soon as I cried just a little bit to wet my damn eyes.

BY THE NEXT MORNING, I WAS IN ONTARIO, HAVING caught a red-eye—oh the irony—home after making a cryptic call telling my folks that I was coming back and needed to talk to them. I also asked that they stay off social media, which wasn't too hard for them, but my brother, on the other hand…

He'd texted me before I left the hotel. Not having the spoons to deal with him, I simply replied that I would tell all when I got to our folks' house. He wasn't pleased with that but eased back to give me room to breathe. I moved through the lobby of the B&B like a criminal, dark eyeglasses, ball cap down to my eyebrows, my path a straight line to the checkout desk and then, out to my waiting ride. All the way to the airport, I sat hunched up, refusing to interact with the driver or anyone else that I came in contact with. I nodded at the people at the airport, grunted at the flight attendant, and ignored the weary-looking man seated beside me. He tried to make small talk, but I pretended I didn't speak English, so he gave up and let me sleep.

The flight was uneventful, and I landed at Toronto Pearson after a quiet five-hour trip where I had fitfully dozed. After leaving the plane, I got my luggage, cleared customs and immigration with ease, and then, took a moment in a men's room to use the bathroom. Locking myself into a stall, I had to fight back a rush of memories of that first hookup with Logan. Even now, with the weight of the world pressing me downward, recalling that brief, but incredible, screw made my dick twitch.

My brother was waiting for me outside in one of the massive parking lots. It was hard to miss his bright yellow minivan. I clomped along, my rolling suitcase bumping after me, and was swept into a hug that nearly winded me. Trying to remain calm, I gave him a fast side embrace, then pulled free, eager to get into the van and away from prying eyes. No one had recognized me yet, but that was sure to change. Canadians knew their hockey. They knew the players, the coaches, the officials, the team mascots, and the guys who shot T-shirt cannons.

"Your eyes look like two piss holes in the snow," Trevor said after stowing my bags in the back of the Sienna.

"Thanks. You're looking good too," I muttered, sliding into the passenger seat, and securing the buckle over my chest.

"I skimmed the sports pages. There are some whispers

here and there with your name attached. Is this what your sudden trip home during the playoffs is about?" He sat with the keys in his hand, so obviously, we weren't leaving yet. He was never able to hide worry or upset well. His dark eyes were sorrowful as he studied me.

"Yes," I whispered, glancing out the window at the happy people trundling by. "Do Mom and Dad know yet?"

"I don't think so, but it's just a matter of time. What I saw was pretty bad, Webber. So much venom out there, and jeez, some guy was even making death threats. Are you seeing a player?"

I shook my head. "Not here, please. Can we just get home?"

"Sure, yeah, of course." He hurried to slide the key into the ignition. I slunk down in the seat, a tension headache creeping up into my forehead from my neck. "You know that whatever happened, we're standing with you."

"Thank you." I gave him a fast peek as he paid for parking. "It's not as trashy as it sounds."

Trevor glanced at me. "I didn't think it would be. I know you." He smiled feebly, then pulled out into traffic. Maybe I had lied a little. My affair with Logan had started off pretty damn trashy, there was no denying that. Fucking in a stall at a club was tasteless. Despite that inglorious beginning, things had changed.

"The death threat?" he pushed.

"Used to those," I said, exhausted. After all, it wasn't the first death threat I'd received from a pissed off, deranged fan, and it wouldn't be the last.

Or maybe it would, given I was basically done with the NHL part of my life.

"Jesus," he said and focused back on the road.

"It wasn't just sex," I blurted as he battled through midday traffic. He shot me a surprised glance but couldn't take his eyes off the road. I had a captive audience. "I mean, it might have started out that way, but...we were really close. Emotionally."

"Do you love him?"

My gaze locked on the bumper of the car ahead of us. Yes, I thought I loved Logan. But to what end? If we loved each other—and he had said he felt he was falling for me —what could possibly come of it? Where would it lead? One of us would have to leave the profession we'd worked so hard to establish. Whoever had to quit would grow to resent the other and then, in the end, we'd split up. And there he or I would be, brokenhearted, alone, jobless...

"I didn't realize that was such a loaded question," Trevor said, his voice slicing through the wallow of woe I was rolling in like a damn elk. My sight flew to my brother. We were halfway home. Christ.

"Sorry, I'm in one of my funks."

"With good reason, but the question still stands. Do you love him?"

"What difference does it make? Our relationship is doomed."

"Ugh, Webber, honestly. You've always been so quick to look at the dark side of everything," he replied with a candor that truly was not needed right now. How about a little sympathy? Did he not realize that my whole life was about to take a header into a cesspool?

"You can fuck right off," I countered. He rolled his eyes and drove in silence. We both exhaled dramatically when we pulled into my parents' tidy little driveway in front of their tidy little house. What a shame their eldest son was about to toss their tidy world on its ear. "I'm sorry about the fuck off comment."

"I know you are. You're distraught. But remember, we're on your side." I looked from the tall oak my brother and I had scaled as kids to Trevor. "It's true. You know how I feel about true love. There is little on this planet that one should allow to come before it."

I blinked to clear away some dewiness. "How are you and I even related?"

"I ask myself that every day." His smile was warm. I wanted to hug him, but my father and mother stepped out onto their little stoop, looks of concern etched on their faces. I gave him an embrace, anyway.

"Are you coming in with me?" I asked, sounding like that scared little boy who had traded his father's Dave Keon autographed puck for a bar of chocolate and ten comic books. I'd asked for my brother to be by my side during that dressing down as well.

"Of course," he said, giving my thigh a tap with the side of his fist.

Mom and Dad both hugged me tentatively, whispering to Trevor as they followed me into the home I had grown up in. I could smell something sweet baking in the kitchen, probably raisin bread, as Mom knew it was my favorite, and the heady aroma of Dad's pipe. The house was unchanged from how it had been for years. A modest split-level in a middle-class town. Two bedrooms upstairs, two baths, and a basement that was too damp to do much with other than store crates of holiday decorations.

We sat down at the kitchen table, my bags toted to our old bedroom upstairs by Trevor, who then joined us as Mom set out coffee mugs and slices of warm bread fresh from the oven.

"Thanks," I said as I took a sip of the strong coffee. Mom liked her coffee to have some kick to it. This pot was full mule. "I wanted you all to be here, so I only had to say this once."

"Webber, I'm sure whatever you have to tell us isn't all that bad," Dad said, getting a nod from my mother.

They had no clue. I took another swig to fortify myself, and then, I began talking. I left out the graphic stuff, obviously. Having to tell my parents that I'd hooked up in a club bathroom with this strange man was bad enough. They didn't need the details. Staring down into the warm blue mug between my hands, I told my family everything. From the beginning to the terrible way things had ended with Logan less than twenty-four hours ago. Christ it felt much longer. It felt as if years had passed…

When the last trembling word left my lips, I drew in a breath, rubbed at my leaking eyes with the tips of my fingers, and glanced at my family. Trevor and Mom both had wet eyes as well, and both reached over the table to take one of my hands.

Dad was harder to read. I could tell he was upset, but was he angry, disgusted, or just ashamed? Or all three.

"Well, I'm not happy to hear that you're picking up strange men in bars, Webber," Mom opened with. "But you know that your father and I are always at your side, no matter what."

Dad nodded silently.

"Mom, he's a grown man who is on the road for months at a time," Trevor piped up as Dad sat back, cold pipe in hand, his gaze locked on me. "I mean, where do you think gay men meet? Hell, Carl and I shared two incredible blow—"

"Your mother does not need to hear about your escapades, Trevor," Dad quickly said, which made my brother blush. "I will say that I understand that men in their prime have certain desires, and that they slake them with people they meet in bars."

Mom gave Dad a hairy eyeball and asked, "Did you slake your desires with bar flies when you were on the road?"

Trevor and I both stared at Dad. He dug into the big pocket on his sweater vest for his pouch of tobacco. Mom tapped her foot on the hardwood floor.

"Of course not, darling," he answered only after his pipe was packed and he had his lighter in his hand. Mom didn't seem convinced, but she let it slide. "And if I had, it would have been before we met because, afterward, I was too besotted with you to even look at another woman."

"Good answer," Mom said, the grim look on her face melting away. "Why don't you take that outside?" She pointed at his pipe. "Trevor and I are going to tidy up."

"We are?" my brother asked.

"We are. And then you're going to get some bread to take home to the boys," Mom told him and that, as they say, was that. Dad and I exited the kitchen through the screen door while Trevor helped Mom clean up the baking mess.

Summer had arrived in Ontario on the wings of songbirds and fluffy white clouds. Dad and I sat down on a glider Mom used for relaxing while reading over her scripts. The next-door neighbor's dog barked, and someone fired up a lawnmower in the distance. Typical sounds in a typical neighborhood. But this day was anything but typical.

"Are you ashamed of me?" I asked after Dad lit his pipe. Smoke curled over his head and was carried away by a warm little breeze that ruffled the new leaves on Mom's rhododendron.

"Of course not, Son. I could never be ashamed of you." I nearly wept in relief. "I am sad that you made such a bad judgment call. You know this is going to be a stain on your name."

"I know."

Dad sighed as if he were weighed down with the weight of the world. I could relate. "I'm upset that you let your libido get the better of you. That's so unlike you. Trevor, I could see acting this way. He's always been the more passionate of you two boys, always haring off after this man or that man, his heart on his sleeve. You were always more self-possessed and more down to earth. More like me, I suppose. Trevor takes after your mother."

"I have her love of all things *Fosse*," I added and got a snort of amusement from my father.

"That you do." He smiled at a robin that was bobbing across the yard. "They got back early this year. Snow was barely off, and the ground was still frozen. Makes it hard to find a worm when the earth is rock hard."

"It...yes, it does." I leaned back into the padded cushion.

"I'm proud of you for telling Dan the truth about you and Logan. You could have lied to cover your ass."

"Thanks," I coughed out, my sight on the robin as it took to wing. I wished I could fly off somewhere. I wished I could fly to Logan because I'd treated him terribly last night. My anxiety had made rational thinking impossible, and I'd said things that were cruel and hurtful.

"Do you love the man?" Dad asked between puffs on his pipe. I let my head drop back to the cushion and stared at the beautiful Ontario sky.

"I do, yes," I whispered in reply.

"Good, that's good. You know when I first met your mother, I was a randy young stag. Chasing every pretty girl who walked in front of me. Don't tell her any of that. She thinks I was a choir boy."

I chuckled. Mom knew the man she had married over forty-five years ago pretty well. He wasn't sneaking anything past her.

"Anyway, when I first met her, she knocked me right off my pins. Turned my world inside out. I never wanted another woman after meeting her, and if someone had come to me back then and told me I couldn't ever see her because it was against the rules of my job..." I rolled my head in his direction and waited as he puffed a time or two. "Well, I'll just say that I'd have been a bricklayer like your grandfather because there was no way on God's green earth that I could have stayed away from that woman. I loved her from the start, and I can hear that you love Logan just as strongly."

"I…do, I do love him, but—"

"No, don't but love, Son. You're either all in or you're all out. I'm sorry that wearing the stripes means you can't be with him. That does sadden me because I know you love it as much as I did. But loving your job is second to you loving someone who completes you. So, if the league decides to can you, then so be it. It's just a job. There are millions of other jobs. There is only one chance to love the person you were destined to be with."

My damn eyes were leaking again. Dad draped an arm around me and turned to kiss my hair just as he had when I was a child. I kind of lost it then. When I got myself together, he was still beside me, arm on my shoulder, making tiny clouds of richly scented smoke.

"I thought you would hate me," I confessed, swiping at my face with the backs of my hands.

"I could never hate you, Webber. You're my child."

God I was a lucky man. Not every queer kid has the kind of parents Trevor and I do. We needed to thank them more. Like every day. Twice on Sundays.

"Thank you, Dad, you're the best."

"Remind your mother of that the next time I forget to take out the trash." That made me chuckle. "So now that we have that worked out for the time being, maybe you should get inside and call Logan."

"I'm not sure he'll even take my call. I was really shitty to him."

"If he's half the man he sounds like, I wager he knows you were freaked out. You've got to try, Son, or all of this will be for nothing. If you have to leave the NHL, at least make it for a good reason like loving someone."

I pressed my lips together, smiled shakily, and kissed him on the cheek. Pushing to my feet, I walked inside, got a slice of bread and a hug from my mother, smiled at my brother washing dishes, and climbed the stairs to call Logan. I wanted to be alone when I had to grovel for forgiveness. A man had to have *some* pride.

Chapter Fourteen

Logan

NICK SINCLAIR WAS DEADLY QUIET. THE OWNER OF THE Boston Rebels wasn't a man to sit quietly. He was fiery and loud, never failed to comment on team affairs with exasperation and lots of eye-rolling and was all about us winning. But today, he seemed to have run out of words, and I knew any chance of getting a contract with the team for next year was off the table. That didn't matter because I'd already decided that hockey and I would part ways after this Cup run. *If I was even part of the Cup run now.* Everyone stared at me. My heart was already broken. Webber didn't want me. Hell, I didn't even want me; and I waited for the inevitable.

"I can't even…" Nick murmured and then, went quiet again. That had been the only words that he'd contributed to this debate behind closed doors. Coach Franks was here, along with Xander in his role as captain, and Marquis, who was the player rep. The rest of us were looking at Nick to do his usual grandstanding spiel about how this latest thing to hit the Rebels was about the last goddamn straw. Instead, we had a deadly quiet version of Nick, and that was a hundred times worse. Awful scenarios spun in my thoughts—right up to the one where Nick sold the Rebels because he'd had enough. He was supportive of the players on his team who were queer. After all, he'd been won over by Xander, even though he'd been cautious at first about having an out-and-proud captain. It wasn't my sexuality that was the issue here. It was what I'd done that was so bad that I'd left him speechless.

He'd never had a player compromise the team so badly.

Coach cleared his throat. "Rumor is that Webber has been asked to stand down."

The room shimmered. I felt sick, and I dug my fingers into my palms. Webber had put everything into his career, and he'd been so proud of being chosen to work during the playoff run. I'd destroyed everything. No, *we* destroyed everything.

"That's wrong," I said. "He shouldn't be the one to—"

"Enough," Nick interrupted loudly, and I subsided. We weren't here to defend Webber. We were here to work out what the fuck I'd done, and if I had a place on the team.

"Sorry—"

"Stop. Fucking. Talking," Nick snapped. "You don't get to sit there and tell the world how they should react." I winced. Not only was he right, but once again, I'd let my emotions get the best of me. So much for me thinking that, if I stayed calm, I could sit this storm out and it might just fade to nothing.

"I *am* sorry." I offered my sincere apology again and winced when he glared at me. I *was* sorry—for what I'd done to the team, and for what I'd done to Webber. We thought we had been so clever, keeping everything on the down low, not telling anyone, just slowly falling for each other in our own time. Instead, I'd ignored the danger signs, and now, look at the position we were in.

Everyone was quiet again, including Nick, who was white-knuckling a sheaf of papers in his hands. Xander wouldn't meet my gaze. Marquis looked confused and torn, and it was Coach who talked instead.

"I've spoken to The Director of Officiating. There's absolutely no question that the last call in the Washington game was correct. There was blatant holding of Rowe's jersey, and the penalty was sound. The decision still stands, and there's no evidence that any call made by Webber in any Rebels game was anything but fair."

I could have told them that because Webber had integrity, and what we were doing—between us—was outside of the game. Surely they should all realize that? *Who am I kidding?* I'm the bad guy here, and there is only one thing I can do.

"I'll retire. Resign. Take the financial hit. Anything that—"

"That's not happening." Nick stood, tapping the papers against his thigh as he paced from one end of the video room to the other. No one interrupted his thinking, and I tried to catch Xander's eye, but he was doing an excellent job of not looking at me. Why would he? I'd single-handedly undermined all the hard work that the Rebels had done to get to the Cup run. I'd only spoken to Xander and Marquis so far, but the rest of the team probably hated me right now, even Austin, who didn't have a bone in his body that wasn't understanding and supportive.

"Logan leaving under his own steam might be the only way," Coach murmured.

Our team owner stopped pacing and pointed a finger at Coach. "How will you fix the team without him? What lines would you put together? Do you have someone you can call up to replace him? Isn't he a sound part of the reason we're even here right now? Losing Dunkirk was about the most fucked up thing to happen to this team, and without Rowe, and him..." he then pointed right at me, "we wouldn't have made it this far."

Fuck. My. Life. The team isn't about one person, and this time when I glanced at Xander he met my gaze steadily. The shit that Nick was spouting had to be the most offensive thing Xander had ever heard.

Xander's expression was tight. "All the hard work *we've* done *as a team.*" He wasn't talking to the room. He was talking to me. "Everything to get here, the sacrifices, the pain, the fact people judge us even more for having a gay captain, and you couldn't stop yourself from fucking a referee until after you were retired?" He was devastated. He knew what love was. After all, he'd found it with Mason, but no one in the room knew how I felt about Webber because I hadn't said.

"I love Webber."

It seemed to be that everyone's silence came before the

storm because each man started talking at once. Only the loudest was Nick Sinclair, and everybody else subsided.

"Love who you love," Nick retorted. "But in all my years in business, I have never seen such a stupid thing as you compromising the integrity of your team and blackening any Cup run, or eventual win, with doubt. You owe the team an apology, you owe me an apology, you owe the damn fans an apology."

Each heated sentence stabbed me harder than the last. I appreciated what I'd done, fallen in love with someone that I should have kept at a distance until at least I was retired, and I didn't have to be told that I owed everyone an atonement.

"I'm sorry. I don't know what else to say. I know I fucked up, and I'll take full responsibility for anything you need me to."

Marquis frowned at me and motioned with his hand to stop me from talking. It must be awful for him to sit there, part of the team whose success was tarnished by my actions, having to back me as my player rep. "Stop talking," he added as if he hadn't made it completely clear.

"No, Marquis, I'm sorry you have to do this, but you don't need to tell me to protect myself when this is on me. I'll take the fines and accept whatever you decide about me still being on the team or making me a healthy scratch or suspending me. But if you think it will work to keep me a Rebel, then I'll block every shot, go to the net every single time, and I will give you everything I have."

Nick turned to Coach. "Can you coach Logan anymore?"

"That's not the question we should be asking." Coach

sighed, and he turned to Xander. "Can you play with Logan?" Xander still hadn't stopped staring at me, and I really wished I could offer him something that would help. But it didn't matter what I promised when the fans and the community didn't want me anywhere near the team. This wasn't a choice anyone could make at team level.

"Without Logan, our lines are seriously compromised," Xander began. "I want us to get the Stanley Cup— it's what we've worked for, what we've sacrificed for, and with Logan as part of the team, we have that chance. But..." he closed his eyes for a moment, and when he opened them, they were bright with emotion, "even if we were to win this year, there'd be an asterisk by our name in people's thoughts like we didn't deserve the win. Fuck. I don't know what to say. I haven't even spoken to the rest of the team, but I know that this isn't something we can spin to make things better."

"I'll play with Logan," Marquis spoke up. "For what it's worth. Everyone makes mistakes, though I'm not saying that I don't hate what he's done. Maybe years ago, he would have gotten away with it because there weren't random strangers taking photos in coffee shops, and his secret would have stayed safe. The same safety queer players have had if they played at our level thirty years ago...anonymity. The question is, how badly do we want the Stanley Cup and how much are we willing to let go to get it?"

"You'd better believe I want that Cup," Nick exclaimed. "The amount of income that will generate for our team—for me—is insane. But whatever people think, I have integrity and reputation matters to me. Of all the things you could have done, Logan, it was not telling us you were fucking a referee. If you'd said something we could have arranged for him not to work our games. Jesus Christ, did you even think about that?"

Grief knotted in my chest. Webber and I had spent so long trying to keep it a secret, we never even thought that maybe the best thing was complete honesty with everyone around us. But then, we couldn't even be honest with each other. I should have told him he was becoming important to me, that I was feeling different about him than any other person I'd ever been with. It wasn't just sex. It wasn't just getting off. It was love, and I should have made him believe that what I was saying was true, instead of worrying about everything else.

"No. It never occurred to me we should be honest with ourselves or with anyone else. I thought none of this through."

My words appeared to floor Nick. He slumped back down into his chair and made this waving motion as if he'd run out of things to say. He wasn't the only one.

Xander cleared his throat. "It seems to me the only way to prove there was no bias is to finish the playoff run and show that Logan is an integral part of the Rebels, is strategically necessary, and that none of the work we've done in the last two rounds was in any way enhanced by a biased referee."

Coach huffed. "But when did it start? Is the entire season compromised?"

Before I could answer with any specifics, Marquis jumped in. "As a member of the team, I agree. However, as a player representative, I know the situation needs to be escalated outside of the team. Up to representation for Logan at a higher level, possibly appointing legal counsel, but that is way out of my remit."

That was a double whammy. Support and distance, all in the same speech, plus the whole concept of legal involvement in case someone out there sued me or the Rebels because they felt our team had, in fact, cheated. How much of a mess had I made? This was horrific, and it wasn't only that everything I'd done was so damn stupid... I'd lost the man I love as well.

"I don't care who sues whom," Xander muttered. "For what it's worth, I hope he stays. I'll talk to the team, but I'm only one vote."

"I'm two for him to stay, and we prove we can do this," Marquis added.

"The hate will be insane," Coach countered, but he didn't indicate either way whether he thought I should stay. "It only takes one player who refuses to skate with him for the entire house of cards to fall down. That's all I have to say about it."

We waited for Nick to give his opinion, but he shook his head; I'd never seen him look so defeated. "Fucking idiot," he grumbled and paused again. "Okay, talk to the team, Xander. I'm leaving the final decision with you." He stood, still clutching the papers he'd walked in with. I saw my name on the top sheet and wondered what his plans were when he came into the office. Was it a list of ways in which he could repair the damage I'd done or a letter of resignation for me to sign? Whatever his intention when he came in, he'd handed the entire responsibility over to Xander, and with a final shake of his head, he left.

"I'll talk to the rest of the team." Xander stood, Marquis copied, and the two of them left without a backward glance. I didn't know what to do. It's not like I was going to be welcome in the locker room while the team discussed what I'd done, and from the way Coach was staring at me, I wasn't welcome to stay here.

"I'll be in my car," I mumbled, but all Coach did was shrug. I left before the shrug turned into more shouting. My car was a safe place. Once I'd shut and locked the door, it was just me, my self-hatred, doubt, and my broken heart. *What the fuck am I doing?* I needed to talk to someone. I tried to connect with my sister, but when the call went to voicemail, I knew she had the phone turned off and was probably at the hospital on duty. Dave couldn't help much. My nieces were too young. I didn't have that many people to call on as friends.

A rental stays nowhere long enough to put down roots.

"Just when you thought you couldn't get any more pathetic," I griped before flicking through messages I'd received. I didn't have a social media presence, but I wouldn't have to search hard if really wanted to find what I was sure would be a ton of hate online. So, it was just me and any text messages or voicemails that I hadn't checked. The messages were from players on teams I'd been with previously. I paused over the one from Dragomirov, Washington's captain and the one person who'd probably resent me the most for what had happened. His message was concise.

You won those games fair and square. The Rebels were the better team on the nights we played. I hope he was worth it, though. Call me if you need to talk.

I sent back a simple reply. *I've lost him. I'm sorry. Thank you.* I didn't expect a reply, but it was as if Dragomirov was waiting for me to respond because the dots started bouncing, and I waited.

You can't lose a person. Find him. Idiot. He'd embellished the message with a couple of middle fingers, and for the first time all day, I actually felt as if I wanted to smile. It didn't last long because what I really wanted to do was sit here and cry.

Find. Him.

I scrolled to Webber's name, but there weren't any messages from him. I imagined him somewhere with his whole life being destroyed and hating that he'd even set eyes on me in that bar. He'd said it was over, but maybe if we just talked, we could at least…

At least what? Admit we loved each other, and that nothing else mattered? Or maybe say goodbye properly? I closed my eyes and leaned back on the headrest, inhaling the scent of leather, and trying to find my center. I wanted to send a message to Webber that meant something, but I didn't know where to begin. What was I feeling right now, not about hockey and my place on the team, but about how much of my heart belonged to Webber? My sister, Dave, and my nieces were everything to me, but my heart had expanded to include Webber.

That is what I should say. That I truly loved him, and that whatever happened, I would wait for him. I could add that I hoped maybe one day when all of this was over, we could find our way back to each other. I'd almost finished typing it out in a notepad so I could copy and paste the exact words I needed to say, but the phone vibrated with an incoming video call.

To my shock, it was Webber's name on the screen. I juggled the phone as I nearly dropped it and pressed the button to connect the call, holding up the phone so I could see his face. My heart stopped, my chest constricted, and all the pent-up emotions inside me exploded out in one word.

"Webber—"

"Stop," Webber said immediately. "Let me get this out."

"But I—"

"Please. I just need to tell you…being a referee and working my way up to where I got meant everything to me, but none of it is worth more than falling in love with you." He blurted the sentence in one breath then visibly winced as he waited for me to reply.

I couldn't breathe. "Sorry?" His words made little sense. The passion in them didn't connect with the pain in my heart, and then he smiled, but it was hesitant and careful.

"I should never have said all those things," he said. "Loving you is more important than my career. I know we've fucked up big time, and maybe we should have been honest with each other much earlier. Maybe we should have told everybody. I don't know what's going to happen next, but I love you. If you don't love me back, I can understand that, but I hope that, one day, you might get back to wanting to be with me and we can—"

"I love you."

"You do?" He sounded so surprised.

"I do."

"Then, I'm coming to you. I'll get a hotel room in Boston, I'll wait for you to get home from road trips, and we can talk about what's next—"

"I might be done already. Xander is in with the team right now."

"Are they going to scratch you? Buy you out of your contract? Shit, Logan, what did we do? We've destroyed everything we worked for because why?"

"We just fell in love without a thought for anything else. Selfish love." I spoke from the heart, and then, it occurred to me he'd said he was going to be getting a hotel room. What was the point of that? "Stay at my place. We'll talk, then weather the storm together, yeah?"

"Okay. I love you, Logan, more than anything."

Sadness consumed me for a moment. I'd met the person who was the other half of me, but then, I'd messed everything up so badly. Still, we had each other. All our mistakes and hesitation in being honest were things we could handle, if we just accepted that we would be together.

"And I love you, too. Please, hurry and get here, yeah? I need you."

Webber smiled at me. "I'm in my childhood bedroom, but I'm already planning flights." He panned the phone, and I could see an old PC in the corner of a tidy room. "I was already coming to you, Logan. It's always going to be you."

A knock on the side window of my car startled the hell out of me, and I glanced sideways to see Xander there. He wasn't smiling, but that meant nothing. I had to go.

"Xander's here. I'm going in with the team. Wish me luck?"

"Good luck. Just remember, I love you, and I'll be back in Boston soon." Webber gave me a soft smile, but I couldn't say any more to him because Xander knocked on the window again. I ended the call and climbed out of the car. Holding Webber's words close to me, I thought, maybe I could face everything and anything.

The locker room was quiet when I stepped in. Every single cubby held a team member in their street clothes, and all of them were staring at me. I tried to get a feel for the tone of the room, and a couple of the guys dropped their gazes, aside from Austin, who immediately stood up and crossed to me, hugging me briefly.

"You should have told us," he said clearly, and most of the team nodded along with that. It seemed they agreed. There was some murmuring dissent toward the back, and I tilted my chin and waited for the criticism.

"Asshole," someone muttered, but Xander wasn't having any of that right now.

"We've all had our say," Xander snapped. "No more. Consensus is that you stay, Logan, and we show everyone that this team got here because we deserved it. We take the next round in four games; we take the final in four; we get to hold the Stanley Cup like it's the easiest thing we've ever done; and we don't show one chink in the armor that surrounds us. We are a team, and what's been said between us before you came in is done. There is no split in how we will focus on playing Toronto at home in two days' time. Eyes front, focused one hundred percent as a team."

"Rebels," Austin said and glanced around at the team.

"Rebels," another voice added. Then another, some less enthusiastic than others.

"Rebels," Austin repeated, louder. After every single man in that room said the same thing, it was my turn, and after the smallest of pauses, I nodded.

"Rebels."

Chapter Fifteen

Webber

I snuck back into Boston as if I were a criminal.

Ball cap, sunglasses, and the collar of my light jacket pulled up to my ears. I felt like some sort of international felon sneaking into the country. In all honesty, I probably didn't need to be so Jason Bourne, but I was trying my best to avoid any hockey fans. No small feat in Bean Town. It seemed everyone was wearing a Rebels jersey. I ducked into a cab outside of Logan International and barked out the address to Logan's place. The cabbie gave me a funny look as if he might know me from somewhere. Thankfully, most refs weren't all that well-known, so I might have been overreacting. I did that sometimes. Case in point...how I came apart when I'd last seen Logan.

I was not proud of myself or my actions. I knew I had hurt him badly, and I hoped to be able to make up for that outburst somehow. Although I wasn't exactly sure how I would ever manage to get that ugly episode wiped off my permanent record of romantic fuckups, I was going to do my best.

"Can you stop here?" I asked when I spotted a small flower shop sitting on a busy street corner. The cabbie hit the blinker, said something about last-minute bullshit, and pulled over. Huh, and I thought only New York cabbies were grumpy. "Leave it running."

I leapt out as the cab pulled to the curb. A light rain was falling. I dashed into the florist, cheeks damp, shoulders speckled with warm summer rain, and moved to the large cooler. A young man in a green apron appeared at my side as I stood staring at the pre-made bouquets.

"Can I help you, sir?"

I gave him a wobbly smile. "I'm in the doghouse." He nodded as if that was a commonly heard thing here, which it probably was. "I need a bouquet that says: please forgive me; I know I'm an ass."

He chuckled lightly. "That's one of our best-selling arrangements." I had figured as much. He presented me with a fat cluster of daffodils, hyacinths, white roses, and some pink carnations. "All of these represent asking for forgiveness. Saying you're an asshole can be written on the card."

I chuckled. "Sold." Five minutes later, I ran out into what was now a deluge, dove into the cab, and got a long, curious look from the cab driver. "Thank you. We can go now."

"Do I know you?" he asked, his sharp dark eyes locked on me in the rearview.

"I don't think so." I stuck my nose into the flowers. He stewed over things for a moment, shrugged a beefy shoulder, and then moved back into traffic. I kept my face hidden in the bouquet until we arrived at Logan's apartment building. I paid the cabbie, tucked the flowers under my coat, and grabbed my lone carry-on bag from the seat beside me. Then, I ran full tilt towards the door. The rain was coming down in sheets. Thunder rumbled overhead. It was mid-afternoon, and the humidity was ghastly, so the rain was bringing some relief.

The door opened. Logan was in shorts and a tank top, his feet bare. He had never looked better.

"Hey," he said awkwardly.

"Hey," I replied. A crack of thunder shook the ground just as a spear of lightning lit up the dark gray sky. A trash can rolled down the street, followed by someone's lawn chair. I jumped a good couple of inches. "Think I can come in before I'm blown back to Canada?"

"God, yeah, sorry. I was just…it's so good to see you." He moved out of the doorway. I hurried inside, dripping water all over his foyer.

"The drowned rat look is a good one for me," I tossed out. He moved far faster than you would think a man his size would move. Before I could speak, he had me in an embrace that was pressing the air from my lungs.

"I've missed you," he whispered beside my wet ear. I felt my throat constrict as emotions that I had been trying to keep in check rallied upward and out. A few tears escaped, mixing with the summer rain on my face.

"I've missed you too," I replied softly, my one arm holding the bouquet hidden under my sodden jacket, shirt pinned to my chest, the other coming up behind him to rest on his lower back. He buried his nose into my hair, breathed in and out, and kissed me under my ear. "I have something for you."

"I thought we would talk first," he replied, his lips still resting on my jugular.

I snickered. He lifted his head to gaze down at me. "No, not that." I stepped back and slowly drew the rather rumpled flowers out. His eyes widened, then he laughed.

"Oh man, I squished them," he said as I handed them over. "You didn't have to do this." He raised the bouquet to his somewhat crooked nose. "I've never had a man give me flowers before."

"Well, it's just a small gesture. Those flowers are supposed to represent asking for forgiveness."

His gaze left the flattened flowers to search my face. "If anyone needs to be forgiven it's me."

I thought to argue, but my clothes were making puddles on the foyer floor. "Maybe we can agree to say that we both fucked things up royally? Also, do you have a towel?"

"Oh shit, sorry." He took me by the hand, leading me to the master bath just off his masculine bedroom. "You can change in here. Even take a shower if you want to warm up. I'll put these in water, and we can have some coffee and talk."

"Thank you." I leaned in to peck his cheek. "I'm so glad I'm here."

He gave me a nervous smile. "I'm glad you're here too."

With that, he left me to change in private. I peeled off my wet stuff, dropped them into the sink, and pawed through my carry-on tote for a change of clothes. I hadn't packed much, as I had no idea if I'd be here for long. The league wasn't exactly killing itself to reply to my emails. I could only assume that I'd be asked to step down soon, which I would without complaint. Well, I'd complain, but not to the league. I'd done the unthinkable. The fallout was mine to bear. On the flight down, I'd been mulling over where to steer my life now that I was a persona non grata in the NHL. There were options, I was sure. I'd always toyed around with the idea of opening a rink for underprivileged youth back in Canada. There were so many kids who couldn't afford to play hockey—many indigenous youths, as well as those who couldn't access the sport—that could benefit from my expertise. I had some money in the bank. Not millions, but enough for a down payment on...well, who knew. I'd only gotten that far.

Shaking off the cobwebs of an overly busy mind and a lack of sleep, I dried off, pulled on some clothes, and made my way back to the kitchen, my wet clothes wrapped in the towel I had used.

Logan was just placing coffee mugs full of steaming goodness on his tiny round table when I walked in.

"I'll toss them into the dryer," he said, so I handed the bundle over and smiled at the flowers in the center of the table. A few were a wee bit wrinkled, but the sweet smell of hyacinth filled the room.

"Are we sitting in here?" I asked as he headed to the dryer.

"No, we can get comfy on the couch," he called over his shoulder dealing with my clothes until the dryer kicked on, running quietly, and he closed the doors. "If you want."

"That's fine." I picked up my mug, enjoying the warmth on my palms. "Isn't this weird?" He cocked his head as he closed the distance. "Us. We're both so awkward with each other now."

"Yeah, I know, but that will go away." He offered me his hand. I took it, and we made our way into the living room as rain beat on the windows. His place was nice, nothing fancy or flashy, and there weren't many personal touches. That was the way of a rental, I was sure. They probably didn't sink their roots in too deep. I sat down as did he, both of us using our coffee cups as distractions for a moment. Thunder boomed outside. I glanced at the windows and then, at Logan, my cup resting on my thigh, the warmth lovely as it radiated through the worn denim.

"Okay, so where do we go from here?" I asked, unsure of even how to open up this talk.

"I'm going to retire," Logan said it with such conviction that I drew back in surprise. "No, it's okay. I've been thinking about it for some time before this whole…"

"Debacle?"

"This whole unexpected love affair began."

Okay, that sounded much nicer. "I'm sorry. What we have is *not* a debacle at all. What happened *because* of what we have is, but not us." I wanted to touch him badly, so I slid my free hand over the sofa to rest on his bare knee. A knee that was scarred and rather puffy looking. The joys of hockey. It was not kind to the human body.

"I know," he said as he placed his warm hand atop mine. "And it's okay to be mad at things. Hell, I'm mad at things. The world, this mess, myself. I seem to bounce between anger, despair, and this overwhelming love for you."

"I know how you feel. At least we're here together now. I shouldn't have been such a dick to you, Logan, and I cannot apologize enough for how I acted. I just freaked out and made you suffer because I panicked. Please know —I promise—I'll never do that again."

He leaned over to steal a chaste kiss. Some of the tension stored in my neck and shoulders began to lessen at the feel of his lips on mine. Maybe, just maybe, he and I could get through this mess and come out on the other side. They say that love can move mountains. We'd see.

"It's okay to be scared. Just don't panic," Logan offered, moving closer so that he could drape his arm around my shoulders. I liked that a lot, so I wiggled into his side, gingerly as we both were holding mugs of coffee. I let my head drop to his shoulder, my eyes locking on the far window over a table with a few knickknacks that obviously came with the place and watched the rain fall. "Do you think the association is going to fire you?" he asked.

"Mm, no, they won't out-and-out fire me. I do have a union and a contract, but that contract has a clause that states they can release me. I suspect they'll just politely suggest I resign, or they'll release me with as much political correctness as they can. It's a potential nightmare for them to fire a gay referee in today's political climate, but I'm not using who I am to push myself to stay. That said, they'd be fully within their rights, but social media would glom onto it and make it into something that it's not. I could appeal, but I won't. They'll give me a nice severance package and pray that I crawl away, never to be heard from again."

"God, that sucks. I am so sorry." He gave my cheek a tender kiss.

"Thanks, no need to be sorry. I knew what the possible penalty would be if I got involved with you." I gazed into those stunning eyes of his, the eyes that I dreamt of every night. Every night that I slept, that was. "As much as this all sucks, I *would* do it all over again, Logan."

"Me too." His lips found mine. The kiss held some heat, but he pulled back after a moment, his brow coming to rest on mine. "I love you. I want a future with you."

My chilly heart warmed. "I want a future with you as well." I sat back a bit, took a sip of coffee, and then placed the mug on the coffee table. "You know that if I leave, you can continue playing, right? The scandal is mostly on me." He shook his head. "No, please, listen. If I leave, things will eventually quiet down."

"Not all of it. We're both in this together. Also, it's time for me to part ways with professional hockey. This whole incident has just made me realize it that much more."

"But, Logan, you love hockey."

"I love you more. And hockey has had me for years. It's been a real bitch of a lover at times. I've had some great moments in this sport, but I've never found anywhere that was really home until I met you."

"That may have been the most beautiful thing anyone has ever said to me," I whispered, cupping his face between my hands, and guiding his mouth to mine.

It hadn't been a kiss that I had intended to deepen. I

just wanted to convey the love in my heart to him. But when his arm came around me, and he gently levered me into his lap, the fire between us that sat banked and always at the ready took hold. His tongue moved over mine, tangling and teasing, as his free hand skittered up under my shirt.

"Coffee…spill…hot," he said as the kiss ended.

I took the cup from his hand, placed it on the table, and then, returned to enjoying his kisses. His hands cupped my ass, pressing me closer so that his erection and mine were side by side. Another rolling volley of thunder shook the windows, but we weren't scared. We were too lost in each other to be nervous about a little thunderstorm. Let the lights go out, let the windows blow out, and let Mother Nature do her worst. We'd survive the tempest, or we would drown. Maybe we'd be blown to Oz. Whatever became of us, we would be together. That was all that mattered.

As the storm raged, Logan and I made our way to his bedroom, leaving a trail of clothes behind like a path of breadcrumbs. We fell into his bed, the storm howling and clawing at the windows unnoticed by the two of us. He moved me to the pillows, sliding one under me. I sighed as his fingers moved over me, into me…

Then his cock was inside me, moving slowly, his body and mine picking up that ancient rhythm. The lights flickered. My fingers dug into the nape of his neck as he rolled his hips, wringing a cry from me that made him move faster. Faster and faster, his hips in syncopation with the thunderhead over the city. He found that cluster of nerves with each thrust. My orgasm was powerful, intense, and perfect. I yelled out my pleasure. The storm hid my cries. Logan gathered me up into his arms as he blew apart, his release coming right on the heels of mine.

"Love you…" he huffed as he filled the condom.

"You too…so much," I breathlessly replied, his belly slipping and sliding in the puddles of my cum.

We lingered in bed for a long time. The storm moved along slowly as our bodies cooled. We whispered and planned, some of those plans pretty grandiose—moving into the castle with Marquis and his prince—and some just plain foolish—setting up a traveling hockey sideshow and charging people to view the two dolts who had blown up two pretty nice careers for love. Why we were suddenly Dickens characters, who knew, but we'd laughed ourselves silly over it, then made love once more. When we finally crawled out of bed and showered, it was nighttime.

We ordered food and ate it in front of the TV, but never turned it on. Instead of losing ourselves in something fictional, we stuffed ourselves on Thai food and began making plans. Serious ones. Ones that we might be able to make come true with enough determination, cash, and love. We were pretty sure we had more than enough of all three, and what we lacked in cash we could borrow. We'd do what we needed to do.

When midnight rolled around, we were in his bed still planning—the windows open, and cool, fresh air moving in to blow away the lingering stuffiness and the last vestiges of any despair or melancholy. Life was funny that way. It liked to rip the chosen path you'd walked along for so long right out from under your feet. Like a bad magician attempting to yank a tablecloth out from under a fine place setting where you were the vase of roses that went ass over flatware to the floor. Sometimes you were shattered, and it looked nearly impossible to fix the broken pottery, but with time and enough love, you slowly began pasting your life back together.

Logan and I had enough love to glue ourselves and our futures back together. There may be some fault lines showing, but that only added character, right?

Chapter Sixteen

Logan

EVEN IF KNIVES WERE ALLOWED IN THE LOCKER ROOM, NOT even the sharpest of them would cut the tension going into the third period of this first game against Toronto. Even with the weight of the home crowd behind us, we couldn't connect to score a freaking goal. Toronto had scored three times in the second period, breaking the back of the game, and leaving us floundering heading into the last twenty minutes.

Coach Franks wasn't happy. "What the fuck was that?" he asked in such a mild tone that you'd be forgiven for thinking he wasn't angry at all, despite using the word fuck. "What's happened to our defense?"

I didn't dare glance over at any of the D-men in case they glared back at me. This was on me. This entire team meltdown was because I'd fucked up. The rest of the team had tried to ignore what happened and pull together, but there was poison among all of us, and it emanated from me.

"Please, for the love of all that's holy, try to get pucks in the back of the goddamn net. And not just our first two lines, I'm talking about all of you, forwards, defense, the only one that seems to have any success tonight is Sergei because I'm telling you now if he wasn't out there guarding the Boston net like a fucking God, there'd be way over three for Toronto's tally. Forty shots on goal from them against our twenty-two? The fuck! Are you all listening to me?"

There were some halfhearted calls of "Yes, Coach" from various skaters, including me, and he went red in the face. I chugged my drink, a bright blue electrolyte injection that I hoped would give me that extra burst of energy for the end of the game. None of us wanted to lose the first game of this potential seven against Toronto, even if they had come into the tournament as one of the strongest teams.

"Look at all of you sitting there with your heads hanging down. Heads up and look at each other, for God's sake." Was Coach throwing an analogy, or was he being literal—should we actually look at each other now? I didn't think I could do that, but Austin elbowed me in the side and whispered my name to encourage me to get with the program. I glanced up, imagining that everybody was going to be looking at me accusingly. We'd had such a good run so far, but their rental had turned out to be more trouble than he was worth. Only no one was actually looking at me, and I didn't know if that was worse until Xander deliberately caught my eye and nodded. I returned the nod, then fixed my gaze on a random piece of wall. Coach was still ranting. "These are your team members. Make sure you remember their faces because you're sure as fuck *not* recognizing them on the ice. Pass. Crisp. Get the pucks on net. We can pull this back. Am I right?"

There was no way in hell any coach could ask members of a professional sports team that question, and not get them riled up with hope and optimism, and this time not one of us hesitated to say "Yes, Coach."

We lined up in the tunnel, and as had become typical, I was right in front of Xander, who always hit the ice last. He tapped my shin with his stick, and I glanced back at him.

"Good work. Don't lose faith in yourself because none of us have."

"Too right," Joachim added, and a couple more voices of the guys closest to me joined the last-minute pep talk. It buoyed me enough that I hit the ice with renewed enthusiasm and ignored the Toronto fans booing us. There'd been a couple of signs with the picture from the café blown up, one of them held by a Toronto fan with wording that suggested we shouldn't even be here. Security assisted with the removal of the poster, but the damage was done, and like wildfire, the heat of social media would burn down my reputation each second I played.

I wished it was just me, and not Webber as well.

From somewhere, we pulled a miracle, scoring three in the space of ten minutes. Two of them from Austin, and one from a lucky rebound off Joachim's skate as he was being shoved away from the net. That pulled us level, and for the first time since my skates touched the ice this evening, I actually felt as if this team might rally a win. When the buzzer sounded, there were three goals apiece. Toronto, angry at themselves for losing the lead, and passionately angry at us for a million different things. When a scuffle broke out a few seconds into the first overtime, there was an inevitability about it. No way to avoid it after they slammed Marquis between the numbers on the back of his jersey and straight into the boards. He was slow to get up, shaking his head where contact had been made, and our big D-men were all over the perpetrator, who dropped gloves and decided that what this shitfest of a game needed was a fight.

Part delaying tactic, part testosterone overload, their player—a skinny, but insanely fast and accurate kid who was only nineteen—and Oscar, our D-man—who was a head taller and a barn door wider—got into it by the net. The fight was over so quickly that if I'd blinked, I would have missed it. The young guy was on the ice, there was blood, and after penalties were assessed for all the things that happened, the momentum of the game changed.

Only this time, it was in Toronto's favor. They were the ones who scored the first goal of overtime after a close call on whether there was goalie interference, and they were the ones who took the win. It was only one game out of potentially seven, we could easily get this back, but it was a subdued group of Rebels who sat in the locker room, some sitting quietly, others voicing their disgust at this call or that call or the fight or a lucky bounce.

Oscar stood up to head for the shower, taking a detour around the logo in the center of the carpet, and passing close to me. "Shame it wasn't your fuck buddy on that last call, eh?" I looked up to see him grinning down at me, and in that second, all thoughts of being sensible vanished, and I saw red. I immediately stood. I wasn't some skinny nineteen-year-old kid from another team. I was almost as tall as Oscar and nearly as wide, and I had years of experience under my belt.

I clenched my fists. "What did you just say?"

"You got an issue with what I said?" Oscar snapped at me.

"Fuck you, Oscar." I shoved his broad chest. I genuinely don't think he was expecting it because he stumbled backward before catching himself and coming straight back for me. He threw the first punch, and it glanced across my cheek as I weaved to the left, and then, I contacted an uppercut to his chin in the fiercest move I'd ever made. The locker room was in chaos, someone was trying to hold Oscar, which allowed me to land more blows before Xander yanked me away so hard that I fell back in my cubby. Marquis sat on me, and he might be all grace and beauty on the ice, but in this moment he was the tough hockey player who was not letting me stand up.

Xander shoved Oscar back and back until there was room between him and me, and then forced him to sit down on the opposite side of the locker room.

"What is wrong with you?!" Xander snapped right in Oscar's face.

"He's fucking a referee, and all I said was it was a shame he wasn't here tonight! We might have won the fucking game."

Xander stood back and away. I could see Oscar's

expression of anger and disappointment, and all the fight left me in an instant.

Marquis relaxed a little on my lap. "Are you done defending Webber's honor now?" he asked.

I nodded, and he wriggled off me to stand, but he didn't go far, probably imagining that I was going to launch myself over the team logo and finish the job that Oscar had started. Xander was laying into Oscar, something he never did normally. He was the captain who had quiet words when he had concerns, and only ever lost his shit with himself, and never with another team member. Leading by example, he tirelessly worked for a better outcome in any game, but he never shouted like this. He seemed to have run out of things to say, glancing back at me, and then, around him at the other skaters, who were pretending not to watch the meltdown.

"We lost the fucking game because we were fucking crap," Xander announced as clear as day. "But we won our way here past Washington because we were better. Nothing to do with calls, bad or otherwise. Now, I'm asking one last freaking time, do we have a problem?"

Silence. A few players glanced at each other, but as usual, it was Austin leading the way in the locker room—a future captain if ever I've seen one.

"No problem here, Cap," he said clearly.

"We won that Washington matchup fair and square," Marquis added. "No problem here."

There was some delay from some guys in answering, but by the end of the shakedown, I think that Xander's words had hit home.

Only, all I could feel was terrible when the realization

hit me. Did they really feel that we won against Washington because Webber had allowed us to? It's fine supporting me and fighting Toronto, but if a single player on this team felt like we didn't deserve to be here, then we might as well decline to play the rest of the games in our Toronto matchup. Not that this could happen, but the rot would get inside our heads, and we'd lose this round in four straight games, and that would be the end of our Stanley Cup journey.

"Webber is a professional," I announced as people moved away, and to give the team credit, they all stopped to listen to me, a game of Chinese whispers telling people that I had said something. When I knew I had the attention of the team, I pushed myself to stand and forced myself to face this. "You don't know him like I do, but he has more integrity in his little finger than most men have in their entire body. He's dedicated to hockey and his career, and all his years of training and his ability to decide outcomes in a split second were always based on fairness and observation and playing by the rules. He didn't give us a free pass. We beat Washington fairly."

There was some muttering, some raised eyebrows, but I hoped that what I said would actually resonate with the team, and who knows, maybe we *would* beat Toronto and get through to the final. Miracles happen.

After all, I'd met Webber, hadn't I?

———

I MADE IT HOME JUST BEFORE MIDNIGHT, PARKING MY Shelby and pausing for a moment to think about how the direction I'd taken in life had given me something even more special than winning a game of hockey. The professional in me was pissed we'd lost tonight, and sad and regretful that the team had failed to believe in themselves because of me and Webber. I don't know if my speech would help, maybe we would just get this far, but I knew that, one day soon, Boston would lift that Cup with Xander as their captain and Austin out in front. Soon, if not this year.

I went into every hockey match telling myself that whatever team I was on was going to win, and between now and our next game against Toronto on Saturday, I really needed to get back into that headspace—the entire team did.

Dragging my tired body out of the car, my knee aching, my cheekbone sore from where Oscar had landed the punch, I shut and locked the car door, taking a moment to admire how pretty she looked in the security light just to give myself time to get my features to rearrange into something like a smile. Then, feeling lighter and looking forward to seeing Webber, I headed to my apartment and let myself in. The inside was in darkness, and for an awful moment, I forgot that Webber might have simply gone to bed, and immediately assumed he'd left me. I flicked on the kitchen light while dealing with the disappointment of him not being here, but a sound from the sitting room made my heart leap. He hadn't left.

Which meant I now had to face him with a bruise that wasn't created in a game.

"Babe, I don't want you to worry, but I may have gotten into a bit of a scuffle post game. Oscar and I had words." He didn't answer, and I imagined him sitting there waiting for me, possibly wearing nothing—never let it be said that I didn't hope. With a smile, I strolled down the corridor, which was brightened by the kitchen lights, already thinking about what I was going to say when I saw him. Only he wasn't there naked and waiting for me.

He was perched on the small coffee table in the gloomy room with a gag tight over his mouth and a knife at his throat.

I froze, taking in the scene, recognizing the young guy sitting next to him, resplendent in Washington red, as the same person who had been collecting the Stanley Cup final player signatures, the one who said I never should have left my old team.

"Webber? Are you okay?" I asked, which was a stupid question, but I knew he'd let me know on a scale of one to fuck if he was terrified or calm, or whether he wanted me to jump into the situation feet first. Webber gave a subtle shake of his head, and as I worked out what was happening, I realized his hands were behind his back, and from the way his shoulders were strained, I guessed they were tied.

"What are you doing?" I asked the assailant. He not only had a knife, but there was a gun in his lap, which must've been how he got Webber in a situation like this. How long had they been sitting here waiting for me to come home? Was Webber scared?

"I knew you'd lose if he wasn't one of the refs," the young guy said with a snarl. I wish I could remember his name. Vince, Veron, or something like it because I've seen enough movies to know that I needed to push past my panic and connect with him. "I knew your team was shit."

"We didn't play so well," I admitted and moved further into the room. It appeared this might have been a step too far into his personal space because the knife moved, and he gripped the gun with his other hand. His eyes widened. He looked as if he was high on something, and that knife was too damn close to Webber's carotid. "Coach wasn't happy that we fucked up," I added, and after a few moments, he seemed to relax.

"You only beat Washington through cheating." He was daring me to disagree, and even though my instinct was to front this completely and leap at him, I instinctively knew I had to play for time.

"Sure. They're a good team and difficult to beat."

What now? My phone was in my pocket, and there was still six feet between me and the knife-wielding man. I imagined getting my phone out to call 911 or moving, but every scenario speeding through my thoughts ended with Webber getting hurt.

"So, you admit this asshole ref let you win?" the kid asked, waving the gun in Webber's direction. My heart stopped. What if the gun accidentally discharged? Or the knife slipped? What was this kid's intention? Were we getting out of this alive? Would I regret it if I stood there and did nothing, and Webber ended up dying? Would I regret moving if it meant that the kid cut Webber's throat?

"Yeah, it was all prearranged," I said with a shrug.

"I knew it!" the kid exclaimed. "I knew we wouldn't have lost without somebody fixing the game, and you were really clever." Was he talking to me or Webber? He loosened his hold on the knife a little so that it was no longer pressing against Webber's skin. I could imagine there was blood there, but in this gloomy half-lit space it was difficult to see. "Austin Rowe must've been in on it to fake that jersey tug and get the penalty. Was it just him or was it the complete team?"

The knife now rested on Webber's clavicle, the hold not so tight, and the kid had placed the gun back in his lap.

"The entire team was in on it," I lied with what I hoped was conviction. "Even Coach. But you know what?"

"What?"

"We all talked about it after the game today, took a vote on whether we should be honest and ask for that call Webber made to be voided." Webber's eyes widened comically, but the young kid moved in his seat, suddenly eager to hear what I had to say. "Turns out there's a rule about that kind of thing. You know, if we backed away, then Washington would take our place." Oh God, the lies were getting more tangled as I talked.

The knife position moved again as the kid shuffled closer to the edge of his seat. This time it rested on Webber's shoulder, and I rationalized that if it slipped, it might cut his arm, but we could deal with that because it wouldn't kill him. *Please forgive me, Webber.*

"For real, Washington can play Toronto?" the kid asked. "And it will all be because of me. That's so cool. Hey, I might even get my name on the Stanley Cup and people can look at it and say, yeah, that's Verne. He knew Boston cheated."

Somehow knowing the kid's name and remembering the day I signed his jersey made this more real, but he was so happy to think that his team might have a second chance, as if that was all that he had in his life. My pity didn't last long, and when Verne glanced at Webber, I took my chance.

I flew that six feet as fast as I could, barreling into Verne and Webber, all three of us falling to the floor in a tangle of limbs. My shoulder hit the ground so hard I heard a sickening crack. I'd lost sight of the gun, but I had both of Verne's hands in mine. Ignoring the pain in my shoulder, I used my weight to pin him to the ground. Just like that fight in the game, even injured, this was definitely one-sided, and I subdued Verne without too much work.

"Are you okay?" I demanded of Webber, and he muttered something behind the gag, crawling backward and rubbing his face on the sofa until the gag slipped down.

"Fuck, I'm glad to see you."

I used one hand to pin Verne, nausea threatening as I moved and the pain in my shoulder peaked, reached for my phone, smashing at the keys until I finally connected to 911. Within ten minutes, cops were at the door, cutting Webber's ties and taking Verne away. In that brief space while waiting, I closed my eyes against the pain, and Webber and I said nothing as if anything we wanted to tell each other was too precious to share in front of someone who wanted to hurt us. As for Verne, he'd stopped trying to get away and was now crying softly, muttering something about Washington and being devastated. I tried not to listen. Hockey was just a game. It wasn't life or death, and this kind of stuff wasn't supposed to happen to me and the people I loved.

I was just a rental.

By the time the cops had left after taking statements, I got a second wind. I pretended I wasn't hurt, refused medical help, downed painkillers, then stalked immediately into the living room where Webber was curled in the sofa corner. He was rubbing his wrists, which were red and sore from where he'd been restrained, and I immediately sat next to him.

What should I say? Should I ask him if he's okay? Should I just hold him quietly? Should I kiss him? The meds were kicking in, and I knew I needed to see a doctor, but right now I wanted to be there for Webber. I fell back on the one mindless thing I could talk about at length. "We lost, but Toronto's defense was insane tonight, and their first and second lines kept up the pressure." I kept talking about the game, inane details of calls and near misses, and the fight after. Slowly, Webber relaxed, then moved closer until, finally, he was tucked under my good arm with his head on my chest.

"I thought I'd never see you again," he whispered.

Now it was my turn to be quiet because all the words I wanted to say would end up with me sobbing like a child.

"I love you." I pressed a kiss to the top of his head.

"I love you too. Thank you for rescuing me," he added the last part, and I knew him well enough to know that he was smiling.

When I thought about the years of loneliness that I had as a rental, always on the road, never settling, I really only had one thing to say to him.

"Thank you for rescuing me first."

Epilogue

Webber

Eighteen months later

I GAVE THE KITCHEN AREA A LOOK THAT OBVIOUSLY TOLD the gathered moms all they needed to know. A dozen sets of eyes smiled at me as I tied an apron around my waist.

"Okay, so I am not a master chef by any means," I confided to the women, and a few men, who were crammed into the food prep area of the almost totally refurbished Moose Cree Ice Hockey Palace. "But I think I can manage to dish up macaroni salad."

"You'll do good," Paul Agoune, the father of one of the forwards who was out on the ice with Logan, assured me. He was a big man. Always grinning. And a savior for Logan and me both, for without his help in finding us this site—a long abandoned fish canning factory right next to the First Nations Cree Reserve on Moose Factory Island in

Northern Ontario—my partner's and my plans would still be on the table back in Boston. "And if you mess up, we'll make you sit in the penalty box."

Everyone thought that was funny, me included. These people had been incredibly gracious and welcoming to the two outcasts who had come to their homes asking if any of their kids might be interested in hockey. The response had been overwhelming. And hectic. So madly hectic. But with help from the community and the helping hands from the Boston Rebels who miraculously never held a grudge against me or Logan, we somehow did what some had said was impossible.

"Right, well, I'll do my best not to crosscheck the macaroni salad," I parried. The parent group was a good gang. Always ready to help out in any way. And most importantly, there were no dirty looks or snide comments. Logan and I had done our best to leave that all behind. Moving up north and taking on this project might have looked like running to some people. I preferred to call it leaving the past as far behind us as possible. Hate messages on social media still found it our way, but it was easier to ignore this far away from everyone. "Speaking of which. Where *is* the salad?"

There were pots of sloppy joe made with moose meat bubbling away on the stove donated by the Rebels organization—the stove, not the moose meat—packages of buns a mile high, huge jars of pickles, poutine about ready to be served, a fruit salsa, sweet potato fries, and a three-bean salad that Paul's wife was stirring as we spoke. Stacks of takeout dishes were ready and waiting on the new counters. This fundraising event for the final step of our new rink had sold so many tickets that we'd had to run out and buy up all the buns on the small island, then head off the island to find more.

"In the walk-in," Marie Biche called over the head of her youngest daughter, who was sampling more pickles than what she was placing in the takeout containers. That girl had a serious pickle love going on.

"I'm on it," I shouted and hurried off to the massive walk-in unit that Logan and I had purchased for the rink. The sound of laughter and chatter followed me into the dark and chilly interior. I flipped on the light, the door closing behind me, shutting out all the chatting. There were shelves full of food, sitting ready in anticipation of our grand opening weekend next Saturday. There were games lined up for four age groups and a concert by one of the local First Nations performers, Wilber Laxado, who was quite skilled on guitar.

I stepped around the shelves, smiling at the huge jars of pickles as the thought of Sarah Biche chewing on a gherkin appeared. Then, just as quickly as that pleasant recollection showed up, a darker one appeared, sneaking out of the dark corners of my mind. I felt that knife on my throat as I stared into the shadowy corner of the walk-in.

"There's nothing there," I told myself, staring wide-eyed at the cases of produce that had just arrived today. Salad makings for the sit-down dinner with the Rebels. That was all it was. No one was lurking behind the tomatoes and lettuce. Still, even knowing that the man who had terrorized me that long, horrible night was now in prison, I felt the crushing wave of a panic attack crashing down over me. I couldn't breathe. I couldn't move. Instead of cold air that reeked of onions, all I could smell was Verne's cologne. The press of the knife on my throat, the pressure against my neck, the raspy growls filled with dire warnings. He'd come out of nowhere. I'd been going to grab a snack to watch the game...cheer on Logan. The kitchen was dark, but the stove hood light had been on. I'd been alone one second, and not the next.

I reached out to grab the shelving unit, but it seemed miles away. The warm trickle of blood from the knife as it sliced into my flesh—lightly, but enough to leave a thin pale line on my skin that I'd carry forever...

"No," I croaked, willing the horror away. I tried to recall the calming words of my therapist for dealing with a panic attack. This was a big one. My knees buckled. Verne was grabbing me now, his sticky hands on my arms, shoving me into the wall, pressing that knife to my throat...

"Web, honey, it's me. Focus on my voice."

I jerked one arm free from the monster behind me, my mind throwing me back into that night, the shadows...

"He was in the shadows," I panted, twisting away.

"I know, but that was him. This is me. Logan. Focus on my voice."

My panic-stricken brain let in that voice. That was safety. "Logan," I gasped, reaching out for him, finding his arms, and throwing myself into his embrace. He held me close, stroking my hair and whispering calming words.

"Good, yeah, that's good. Breathe in and out. Nice, yeah, that's great. Five breaths in and then five out. Good, so good," Logan whispered as he held me. The man was well familiar with these episodes. I'd had them nearly every night—and during the day as well—right after the event as Dr. Lowry, my therapist, had coined it. It was the good doctor—and Logan's presence throughout the aftermath of that time—that had gotten me through it.

"Oh…shit," I coughed, my pulse thundering through my ears, the lingering smell of Verne's cheap cologne and his sweat still clinging to the inside of my nose. I buried my face into the smooth material of his sweater, my fingers balling up the jersey as I worked on pulling in air. The breathing exercises helped. "Damn…it's been so long since that's happened."

"Yeah, that's okay, though. Doc said that it's normal to go months, even years, and then something will set off an attack. You did so good." He brushed some hair from my face, pulling back to study me. I tried to smile, but it was a poor attempt. "Yeah, there you are, back from the dark place."

"I'm here," I croaked, letting my cheek rest on his heart. Always so strong that beat was. Steady, sure, unwavering. No matter what the world threw at us, he was always the steadfast one, which was good because someone had to be. Christ knew it wasn't me. I'd been a wreck for months after the event at Logan's old home. The press had gone mad for the story, dredging it up over and over and over for months. Detailing everything about my attacker, showing his face all the time, shouting about his past. Did the media not care that I had to see that face every day? Didn't they give a shit that maybe I was trying to get that visage out of my memory banks? Not that that would ever happen, but holy hell, did they have to talk about it daily? I came to realize that the press didn't care about victims, no matter how much lip service they doled out. If they did, they'd not splash the perp's face all over the place. They'd not follow the victim and his boyfriend everywhere, yelling out questions, snapping pictures, and making crude suggestions. Love triangle gone astray. The bastards. All they cared about were the headlines. Grab the clicks. Can we get the victim on the set? "Shit, I feel so stupid. All the team parents are here, the Rebels are here, and I go and fall apart."

"Hey, it's fine. You didn't fall apart. You were already whispering your mantra when I came in to check on the macaroni salad you had been sent to find." He cupped my face. His hands were big, warm, and rough. Cold air blew over us, but he didn't shudder. He was probably overheated from being on the ice with the kids and the handful of Rebels that had come up for the big event. Austin and his boyfriend, Xander and his partner, Joachim and his love, Marquis and his prince. A prince! Right here in Moose Factory, Ontario! Even the tribal elders had been impressed with that, inviting all of us to their elder Christmas dinner in two days.

"I was? Oh good." I didn't recall my breathing mantra kicking but it had. I hadn't spoken to my therapist for a month. Perhaps I needed to find a new one here on the island. I would do that right after I got out of this damn walk-in cooler. Well, maybe not right after. There were going to be hundreds of people lining up for the sloppy joes they'd ordered. Hell, there were hundreds here now, out in the rink, spending time with the professional players that had been so instrumental in this program. "Good. Okay, I'm…better." I drew in a long, shaky breath and then lifted my cheek from Logan's thumping heart. He smiled down at me, calm and cool. Well, we *were* in a walk-in, but he was unflappable.

During all the chaos of our affair being discovered and then the night of terror, he had been a rock. He'd stood tall as the Rebels had fought their way to the final round and won the battle for the Stanley Cup. Logan's name was on that Cup, but he didn't join in with the team celebrations despite being asked to by nearly every member of the team. He cited the fact he'd had two separate operations on his shoulder—but really he was preoccupied with how our relationship was being perceived, not to mention my meltdown after the attack. People still blamed us for Washington leaving the competition, and for Boston ultimately going all the way and winning the Cup, and he didn't want to take the shine away from the success of his old team.

"How are *you*?" I asked him.

"I'm good. Cold, a little, but good. The kids are still jabbering at the guys. They had a million questions, and it's not often pro players come this far north to spend time with some kids." But the Rebels had come without us even asking. They'd offered as soon as Logan had texted them with the idea, way before we'd left Boston behind. Both the players and the organization had donated time and money to the cause. Logan and I had also invested heavily, and the payoffs were being seen already. It might take a few years for the older kids to make a splash in the draft, but there were a couple of players that were going to be something big in about four or five years. "You're trembling." He began rubbing my biceps. "You want to go back to the cabin to rest?"

Our little log cabin home was nothing fancy, but it was ours. Situated on the outskirts of the Cree Reserve lands, we'd bought it from an old trapper who was looking to head to warmer climates. It had needed lots of work as it was pretty much a trapping shack, but we dove into it, hiring craftsmen from the reserve. It was homey and warm and filled with love. Who needed mansions or castles? Not us. We were done with the big city rat race. Logan liked to joke that we were just a couple of old hermits, just like Jean Claude, whom we'd bought the cabin from. I always countered that if we had to live off what we trapped, we'd be dead in a week. Logan enjoyed that whenever I said it. Mostly because it was the truth.

We hadn't run, we were happy and building a brand-new life.

Thankfully, our neighbors kept us well-stocked on fish and game. We'd never go hungry. The hockey moms would make sure of that. They'd not want their head coach and senior official to pass out on the ice from lack of food.

There was a soft rap on the door before it creaked open. There stood Paul, his hands over his eyes.

"Are you two being naughty?" he asked. All the ladies behind him tittered. You get caught making out one time in the storage closet…

"No, it's too cold to be naughty," Logan replied, pulling me to him once more. "We'll be right out."

"Okay and bring that salad. There are folks lined up at the front doors." Paul eased the door shut, and the fridge grew darker again, the lone bulb throwing the chilly area into those creepy shadows. I took a moment to gather myself and draw in a long, deep breath of Logan Mackie.

"I'm good," I said. He drew back to study me, head tipped. "I am. I'm good. It was just a fright is all." He seemed unconvinced, but slowly released me, his hands lingering on my shoulders. "We have hungry hockey fans and players to feed. We better get out there before they knock down the doors and storm the place looking for sloppy joe and poutine."

"You're amazing, you know that, right?"

No, not really. He was the amazing one. He and our families had rallied behind us when the shit had hit the fan. And he and the Rebels' organization had done what they could and donated hundreds of thousands of dollars to our dream. Logan liked to say that he thought the Rebels' owner was tossing cash at us for two reasons. One, it was incredible publicity, and two, it got us the hell away from Boston. He was probably right on both counts. The owner and the players had flown all the way up here two days before Christmas. Each and every one of the men out there in a Rebels jersey was an amazing human being. Kind, giving, accepting. Just like the people here on our cold little island.

"I'm okay. *You're* the amazing one," I countered, and he smiled.

"No, *you're* the amazing one," he replied and stole a sweet kiss. That helped to warm me up and chase away the lingering memories of the darkest of times.

"No, *you're* the amazing one," I parried and so on it would go until we both admitted that we were both amazing and patted ourselves on the back.

The din of male voices grew louder. The players were now in the kitchen. "Okay, the guys are looking for food," I said and gave his scruffy cheek a pat. "We'd better get the salad out there before they start eating the dry buns."

"That totally sounds like something Austin would do," he said, then chuckled. His face turned serious as I spun to locate the big bowls of macaroni salad hidden behind the condiments. "Are you sure you're okay?"

I peeked back around the shelves and nodded. "I'll always be fine as long as you're nearby."

His smile lit up the walk-in just as it had my life. No matter how dark the times, as long as you had your other half nearby, you could weather anything.

Even feeding ravenous hockey players.

THE END

Hockey Series' from RJ Scott & V.L. Locey

Harrisburg Railers

Owatonna U Hockey

Arizona Raptors

Boston Rebels

LA Storm

Chesterford Coyotes - Young Adult

Free Reads

Please note - in all of these free stories, there will be some spoilers for the main series books.

Railers Short Stories

Volume 1 | Volume 2

LA Storm

Sparkle

The Colts - AHL Short Stories

Pucks & Percentages

Breakaway

Making the Save

Standalone

Waiting for Christmas

Harrisburg Railers

When hockey wunderkind Tennant Rowe meets his new coach, he knows he's in trouble. Jared Madsen is nine years older than Tennant, impossibly attractive, and — worst of all — his brother's off-limits best friend. Is their chemistry worth the risk?

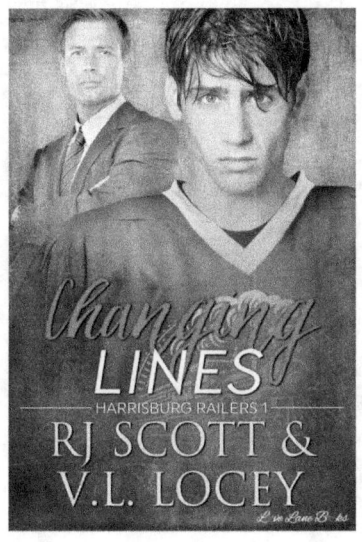

Changing Lines (Railers 1)

Can Tennant show Jared that age is just a number, and that love is all that matters?

The Rowe Brothers are famous hockey hotshots, but as the youngest of the trio, Tennant has always had to play against his brothers' reputations. To get out of their shadows, and against their advice, he accepts a trade to the Harrisburg Railers, where he runs into Jared Madsen. Mads is an old family friend and his brother's one-time teammate. Mads is Tennant's new coach. And Mads is the sexiest thing he's ever laid eyes on.

Jared Madsen's hockey career was cut short by a fault in his heart, but coaching keeps him close to the game. When Ten is traded to the team, his carefully organized world is thrown into chaos. Nine years his junior and his best friend's brother, he knows Ten is strictly off-limits, but as soon as he sees Ten's moves, on and off the ice, he knows that his heart could get him into trouble again.

Changing Lines

Harrisburg Railers (Hockey Romance)

Railers Volume 1 | *Railers Volume 2* | *Railers Volume 3* | *Railers Volume 4*

Meet the men of Owatonna University's hockey team

Ryker (Owatonna U, 1)

Ryker

Ryker is hockey royalty, Jacob is a poor country boy. Can two vastly different people find common ground and become the men they want to be?

Ryker comes from a long line of championship-winning hockey players. Playing college hockey to develop his game is his only focus, and nothing will stand in the way of him working to become the best player. He has no room for relationships, people who point out his flaws, or anyone who calls him on his dreams. He certainly has no place for love, and meeting Jacob is nothing but a useful distraction on the side. After all trying to get his Owatonna Eagles teammate into bed is less work and more play. When tragedy rocks his family, his charmed life crumbles, and the only person he can turn to is the same one who claims to hate him.

Jacob Benson has only known hard work and stifling conservative values his whole life. Born and raised in the small rural community of Eden Crossing, Minnesota, he's the only son of a hard-working but struggling dairy farming family. Jacob is using his skills in hockey to finance his way to an agricultural science degree. These four years at Owatonna U. will probably be the only time he has to enjoy life, gain acceptance about his sexuality, and live openly before his inevitable return to the farm. Running into a pretty rich boy like Ryker Madsen is putting a damper on his enjoyment of life away from home. Ryker's flip, conceited, carefree attitude grates on Jacob's every nerve. So why, if Ryker is everything he dislikes, does he want nothing more than to explore the sinful dreams that his annoying teammate stars in every night?

Ryker

Owatonna U Hockey (Hockey Romance)

1. Ryker
2. Scott
3. Benoit

Coast to Coast (Arizona Raptors 1)

Coast To Coast

When opposites attract, this bottom-of-the-league team will never be the same again.

A stipulation in his father's will forces Mark back into the arms of a family that disowned him and leaves him one-third owner of a hockey team facing financial ruin. He doesn't even watch hockey, let alone like it, and wants nothing more than to head back to New York. Then there's the new coach, a stubborn, opinionated, irritating man with superiority issues and questionable music taste. Butting heads with Rowen becomes the new normal, but it comes with passionate debate and an all-consuming lust.

Challenged to rebuild one of the worst teams in the league into a future cup contender, Rowen can't pass up the opportunity. Never in his twenty years of hockey has he ever seen a team managed so badly or coached players overflowing with resentment and bigotry. Yet there's something about this team and this city that compels him to roll up his sleeves and start dismantling. If only Mark, one of three siblings who now own the Raptors, wasn't so damned rock-headed yet so damned appealing his job might be easier. It doesn't look like either is willing to give in, but one night in a dark, desert hotel changes everything.

Coast To Coast

Arizona Raptors (Hockey Romance)

1. Coast To Coast
2. Across the Pond
3. Shadow and Light
4. Sugar and Ice
5. School and Rock

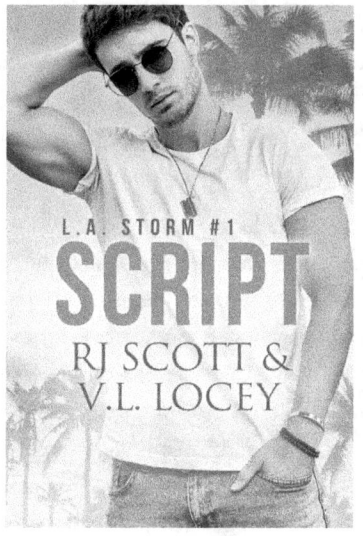

Script (LA Storm, 1)

Script

Hollywood A-lister Finn might be Canadian, but he needs Cameron to show him how to hockey.

Actor Finn Kerrigan is at a crossroads. After growing up a soap star, then starring in a hugely successful trilogy of action movies, he's finally given the chance to read a heartfelt and passionate script that could change his life forever. The role would be enough for people to see him as a serious actor, and maybe even win him an award or two (and no, a golden raspberry award for his action movies doesn't count). Once established as a serious actor he's sure he can come out of the closet and finally live his truth. When he lies to get the part of a hockey player on a struggling team, he suddenly has nowhere to hide. He might be Canadian, but the last time he skated he was ten, and no, he doesn't have hockey in his blood. With only a month until filming starts, he about to be exposed, but partnered with a player who's supposed to be giving him tips, he doesn't realize how many of his secrets will come to light. Falling in lust, one heated kiss at a time, is inevitable, but giving Cameron up at the end of the shoot could break his heart.

Cameron Chavkin is the face of the LA Storm. And the body, and the hair, and the smile. He's at the prime of his career, men and women want to be with him, and he's skating better than he ever has before. His house sits next to a famous rock star's mansion, his garage is filled with expensive cars, and he's even been asked to mentor a once-famous actor in a new hockey movie. Life is pretty sweet. Until the bad boy of hockey meets Finn, a man on the edge with more secrets than Cameron has endorsements. Knowing better than to get involved, Cameron is swept up despite himself, and when it's time to say goodbye to the Storm's most eligible bachelor is finding it hard to follow the script.

Script

LA Storm

1. Script
2. Second
3. Shield
4. Spiral

Off The Ice (Chesterford Coyotes, 1)

Off The Ice

A coming-of-age love story with high school, hockey rivalry, friendship, family, and coming out.

Soren's life changes in an instant when he and his younger brother are adopted by hockey royalty. Making sense of his new life is hard enough, but when he's enrolled in a private school it means facing a whole new set of problems. Navigating friendship, family, and hockey is one thing, but being attracted to the boy who vexes him is a whole new thing.

Felix has a reputation to protect. He's the kid who seems to have everything but looks can be deceiving. Spinning lies about his perfect life, he's created a fantasy world that even he has started to believe. Only, it's not long before everything crumbles, all of his pretty lies are revealed, and only his closest rival sees through his pain and stands by him.

Fighting is easy, friendship is hard, but love is everything.

Off The Ice

Chesterford Coyotes

1. Off The Ice
2. On Thin Ice
3. *Dance on Ice*

Also By RJ Scott

For a full list of ebooks and links please scan the code above or
visit rjscott.co.uk/rjbooks

Meet RJ Scott

RJ discovered romance in books at a very young age and realized that if there wasn't romance on the page, she could create it in her head. With over one hundred and fifty books published, she is a full time author of gay romance.

She lives and works out of her home in the beautiful English countryside, spends her spare time reading, watching films, and enjoying time with her family.

The last time she had a week's break from writing she didn't like it one little bit and has yet to meet a box of chocolates she couldn't defeat.

www.rjscott.co.uk | rj@rjscott.co.uk

NEWSLETTER - rjscott.co.uk/rjnews

facebook.com/author.rjscott

x.com/Rjscott_author

instagram.com/rjscott_author

amazon.com/author/rj-scott

bookbub.com/authors/rj-scott

goodreads.com/rjscott

pinterest.com/rjscottauthor

Also By VL Locey

For a full list of ebooks and links please scan the code above or
visit vllocey.com/stories-from-vl-locey

Meet V.L. Locey

V.L. Locey loves worn jeans, yoga, belly laughs, walking, reading and writing lusty tales, Greek mythology, the New York Rangers, comic books, and coffee.

(Not necessarily in that order.)

She shares her life with her husband, her daughter, one dog, two cats, a flock of assorted domestic fowl, and two Jersey steers.

When not writing spicy romances, she enjoys spending her day with her menagerie in the rolling hills of Pennsylvania with a cup of fresh java in hand.

vllocey.com
vicki@vllocey.com

Newsletter - vllocey.com/newsletter

facebook.com/V.L.Locey
x.com/vllocey
instagram.com/vl_locey
bookbub.com/authors/v-l-locey
goodreads.com/vllocey
pinterest.com/vllocey